DAMAGED

THE BILLIONAIRE'S SECRET CLUB SERIES BOOK 5

C.C. PIPER

© Copyright 2020 - All rights reserved.

It is not legal to reproduce, duplicate, or transmit any part of this document in either electronic means or in printed format. Recording of this publication is strictly prohibited and any storage of this document is not allowed unless with written permission from the publisher except for the use of brief quotations in a book review.

This book is a work of fiction. Any resemblance to persons, living or dead, or places, events or locations is purely coincidental.

ABOUT THE AUTHOR

C.C Piper is the collective pen name for two young guys who happen to absolutely love romance. The pair have been reading romance novels for years and will rarely be seen without a romance novel in their hands, or on their Kindle close by.

After swapping notes, the pair decided to try their hand at writing their own romance novels. Over the last few years the duo have been working tirelessly to improve their writing skills and to publish unique and enthralling stories that readers can really connect with.

Come join our Facebook Group if you want to interact with us on a daily basis, win FREE giveaways, and find out when new content is being released.

Join Our Exclusive Facebook Group NOW By Clicking Below!

https://www.facebook.com/groups/ccpipersreadergroup

CONTENTS

1. Jessie — 1
2. Trevor — 9
3. Jessie — 17
4. Trevor — 26
5. Jessie — 37
6. Trevor — 45
7. Jessie — 55
8. Trevor — 62
9. Jessie — 71
10. Trevor — 77
11. Jessie — 93
12. Trevor — 101
13. Jessie — 118
14. Trevor — 134
15. Jessie — 149
16. Trevor — 165
17. Jessie — 177
18. Trevor — 204
19. Jessie — 216
20. Trevor — 225
21. Jessie — 238
22. Trevor — 247
    Epilogue - Jessie — 265

OFF LIMITS

1. Alaina — 273
2. Mason — 284

1

JESSIE

OCTOBER

I glanced up at the large circular clock on the cement block wall. Damn. Ten minutes left. I hated essay tests, even though I loved Student Engagement, the subject of the class. Once this semester was complete, I'd only have one more semester 'till I'd have my degree in Early Childhood Education.

My dream.

Becoming a teacher would allow me to do two things. One, make a difference in the lives of children. And two, have some way to support myself financially. Not that pay for teachers was fantastic or anything, but it would be enough to survive on. Well, as long as I was careful. And since careful was my middle name, I knew I could swing it.

Besides, I was sick of living in survival mode. All. The. Time.

Technically, I already was a teacher. I had been making an *almost* living as a fitness trainer and Zumba instructor for the past three years, so being in charge of a class would be nothing new to me. Of course, teaching adults was far different than herding five-year-olds. But I looked forward to this upcoming change in my life just the same.

Now, if I could only get there.

I wrote and wrote and *wrote*. Part of my scholarship package required maintaining a certain grade point average, and because my life tended to be tumultuous, sometimes that proved to be a challenge. It's difficult to concentrate when you don't know where your next meal might come from or if you'll have a roof over your head that night.

Being homeless my freshman year had nearly caused me to drop out.

Thank God for Ashley Winter. Ashley had been one of my friendly acquaintances in high school. Since that time, she had become my BFF and roommate. Like a lot of teenagers, I'd had a large loose band of fair-weather friends back then.

The types of girls who liked to gossip and borrow your lipstick, but when the shit hit the fan, sort of disappeared.

I hadn't realized it at the time, but that's exactly who I'd surrounded myself with. Surface level personalities without much substance. So when things went south in my life—and by south I mean straight to hell—the true measure of these friendships was tried and tested big time.

This meant that after the ordeal I'd faced, my posse went from eight girls to one.

Ashley, although she'd been on the outside of that circle, had ultimately become the one that stayed.

Not that I could blame the other seven, really. After being ejected from the apartment I'd grown up in, I'd been alone and in a pretty sorry state. It wasn't easy to be kicked out of your childhood home by your own flesh and blood. Regardless, though, who wants some blubbering teenage girl taking up long term residence on their couch?

The fact that I was pregnant and hormonal—not that I'd told anyone—hadn't helped much, either.

The first night, I slept out under the stars in a local park. I sobbed the entire time. Then, since that experience was scary enough to not repeat it, I went from one friend to the next until I wore out my welcome on each. Some friends let me stay a week, some a weekend, and with one, only a few hours. All of them said *sorry Jessie, I didn't sign up for this*, and showed me the door.

Needless to say, the slumber party invites came to a screeching halt after that.

I went from popular, good-time Jessie to "that Jessie Souza chick is like, *such* a drag," overnight. I had to grow up instantly, which at seventeen proved hard. Somehow, I managed to graduate that spring, but I didn't walk the stage. I couldn't afford the extra expense of a cap and gown.

During my first week of college, I miscarried. The first thing I felt was devastation. Then, I felt relieved to not have the responsibility of another mouth to feed. *Then*, I was consumed with guilt for feeling relieved. What kind of sadistic monster would experience relief, no matter how brief, over the loss of her baby?

Me. That's who. I inadvertently became as bad of a parent as my own mother. And that shit was unforgivable.

"That's time, everyone."

Fuck. Fuckity fuck fuck.

I had one more question to answer. The room came to life around me, yanking me back to my current reality. Shuffles of backpacks and the clomps of shoes filled my ears as wafts of various perfumes and colognes clogged the atmosphere—except for that one dude who reeked of weed. Still, I kept my head down and rushed to finish. *Just a few more sentences. I need to pass. I* have *to pass.*

"Ms. Souza," called my professor, once everyone else was gone.

"Yes, Professor Shirley?"

Professor Shirley was my all-time favorite teacher. Ever. She had short black hair that always looked windblown, and dark, discerning eyes. She was also even more petite than I was, and considering I was five foot three while wearing two-inch heels, that was saying something.

I fully expected her to tell me to wrap up my last word and bring her my examination paper. Instead, she collected the tests into a rudimentary stack and came to stand next to me. I stared up at her and was met with a soft, compassionate gaze.

"I'm going to go get a quick cup of coffee. Can I assume you'll be waiting on me when I get back?"

"Absolutely."

She nodded, then left, giving me an additional fifteen minutes to round out my response. It was the exact amount of time I needed. Unfortunately, staying over meant I was now running late for the gym. My workplace was ten blocks away from the university. After handing in my paper, I threw on my jacket as I ran for the door. At the threshold, though, I turned back.

"Thank you," I whispered, but due to the acoustics, even that low sound echoed through the cavernous classroom.

Her smile reflected in her eyes. "Don't mention it."

Who knew a college professor would end up being kinder and more generous than the woman who'd given birth to me?

But all that crap with my mom was... whatever.

I didn't like to think about how my life had imploded or why. I had to keep on keeping on just like I had for the past three and a half years. So I would.

I jogged through the crowds of Brooklyn, skirting down leaf-strewn sidewalks and across busy intersections without stopping. It was a good thing all the lights changed just as I approached them. A rare bit of good luck. Because it was October, the air was crisp when I inhaled, but I didn't pay the weather much mind. New England was known for its cool, colorful autumns, and I liked experiencing all four seasons. At least, as long as I didn't have to sleep outside in them.

By the time I arrived at the gym, my students were stretching out their hamstrings and calf muscles along the back wall. Taking just a second to regain my breath, I turned on some loud percussive music and changed into my workout shoes. Then, clapping with the beat, I faced the mirrored wall, just like my students. Getting into the appropriate rhythm, I demonstrated an easy punching step and began the class.

"Jessie, sweetie, can you come into my office?" came the saccharin voice of my direct supervisor, Lance.

Red flag. He only called me "sweetie" when he had bad news.

"Yeah ..." he said slowly when I stood in front of his desk,, reminding me of that jerk of a boss in *Office Space*. "You see, the thing is, the enrollment levels in your classes are down. So effective immediately, we're going to cut back your hours, okay?"

"By how much?" I asked, a sinking feeling taking over my gut.

"Oh, by about ten. You'll go from thirty to twenty a week, so it shouldn't be too awful."

Maybe not for him, but for me that type of cut meant I couldn't make either my meager portion of the rent—Ashley paid sixty percent to my forty as it was—or pay for school. I could only afford one and not the other.

Dammit.

"Lance, I really can't afford for you to do that." He threw me an expression that seemed torn between a fake smile and a real grimace.

"Sorry, sweetie, but that's the way the cookie crumbles sometimes."

Was he seriously bringing up stupid platitudes right now?

"Maybe if your numbers increase, we can find a couple more hours for you in the future," he suggested, not sounding very encouraging since his eyes were on his phone.

"Fine."

I'd forgotten a change of clothes, so I hopped aboard the B train feeling stinky and sweaty. I should've known my tiny moment of good luck wouldn't last.

2

TREVOR

I ain't gonna lie, going from the Big Easy to the Big Apple required some adjustments. Several of them, in fact. The main one was acclimating myself to the temperatures going colder earlier. Weather down in New Orleans was mild year 'round. Granted, we had our little cold snaps now and again, but right now, even though it was still October, it was forty degrees. To me, that was downright chilly, and it was only going to get chillier.

Mostly, though, I liked being here.

NYC has this frenetic energy, a super-fast pace, you know? A certain vibe, as my Nana would call it. Nana always was into mysticism. She was Cajun, and as superstitious as anyone I knew. But then coming from a part of the world known for its occult practices and voodoo made believing in things others might not more likely. I should know.

I'd been raised not to walk under ladders or to break mirrors. I couldn't even say how many times I'd been freaked out as a kid by the rocking chair on my parent's porch rocking all by itself. That sort of thing didn't bother me so much anymore, but I did still put stock in my instincts, in feeling situations out and backing away from circumstances that didn't feel right.

I might not be able to explain it, but I knew there was more to this life than meets the naked eye.

It was that instinct that caused me to move here in the first place. I needed a fresh start.

Not that I didn't love Louisiana. My family were all from there, and so was my best friend, Jaxson Liddell. I'd been here for six months now and I missed them all terribly. I missed the warmer temps, too. But I didn't feel like New Orleans had the same opportunities for me that Manhattan did. So I weighed my options and did the whole list of pros and cons. Then, I went exclusively with my gut and hopped aboard a plane.

For the first time in my life, I felt like I might actually get the chance to step out from beneath Jax's shadow.

I even told him as much, as tactless as that might've been. But I've never had much of a filter and lying about my feelings seemed wrong. So I explained that I wanted to strike out on my own. Make a name for myself that had nothing to do with Liddell Industries, his family's billion-dollar tech firm.

The name Liddell held a lot of clout at home. Few people from that neck of the woods wouldn't know it. I wanted the same for myself. I wanted the name recognition and respect. I wanted success that was exclusively my own.

I'd worked for Liddell Industries my entire adult life, and yet I could never seem to accomplish the sort of recognition and prestige I'd aimed for. Jax had been away for four years in the company's London office, and I thought I'd made some headway in that time. And I had. I received three separate promotions and believed I'd covered some important ground.

But the moment Jax returned, much of what I'd done seemed to mean nothing. Everyone deferred to him automatically and not only because of his last name. It was because of the qualities my best friend had. His steadfastness and strength of character; his decency and sense of fair play. His father had ruled the place with unyielding ruthlessness, but Jax took the opposite approach. Liddell Industries had flourished under it, too. It was amazing to watch.

Yet, staying there meant I'd never be top banana. And maybe this was selfish, but I wanted my own piece of the pie.

So when an opportunity arose to become an investment banker on Wall Street, I took it. I'd had my nose to the grindstone so hard over these past few months that I discontinued every other aspect of my life. I hadn't gone home to visit. Hadn't engaged in any nights out with friends. Hadn't dated. I'd made work my only priority. And now that I lifted my head from my metaphorical ledgers, I realized something.

I was lonely.

I'd never gone so long without my family or my friends. I'd also never gone so long without a woman in my bed. That was another advantage Jax had over me. He was now a happily married husband and father, even if his initial escapade into fatherhood had been unknown to him. His parents had hidden the truth of his girlfriend Roxy's pregnancy, the sickos; still, he wound up with the girl he'd always wanted. The girl he'd always loved.

But I knew better than to wish for that. It was one thing for me to go after money. With the right investments and know-how, money would accumulate and grow. It wasn't even that hard to do as long as you were willing to put in the time and effort, especially since I already held an MBA. But love? That was a whole other species.

There was no rulebook when it came to love, no strategy. Sure, you could strategize sex and dating, but love? That was a beast I didn't think possible to tame.

You just had to be lucky. To be at the right place at the right time. Both the people involved needed to be right for each other, too, and that was tricky as all hell. Possible but massively difficult. Especially for me.

My problem was I had certain, shall we say, proclivities when it came to sexual gratification. I could only ever feel satisfied when my bed partner was okay with engaging in some unique forms of play. Jax knew this because he approached his sex life in a similar way. As I stared out the window of the forty-story skyscraper and into the night, I chuckled to myself. Jax fell hook, line, and sinker for the notion that I had some perverted fire fetish that I indulged in.

But the joke was on him. Can you imagine? What would such a thing even *look* like?

"Hold still, darlin', as I set your long lovely hair aflame."

I mean, *damn*. Sadomasochism, indeed.

No. I wasn't into anything that extreme. But I enjoyed being a dominant in the bedroom. I liked to have control and be in control. I liked to give orders and have them followed without question. Well, *like* might not be a strong enough word. I had a difficult time getting off without those measures being taken. I didn't just like being in charge. I *needed* to be.

Yet, in my experience, the average woman of dating age often wouldn't agree to such things. Which left me in a quandary. I needed some X-rated time with a woman. Like, ASAP. I just wasn't certain how to go about tracking down a submissive here in the city that never sleeps.

Surely, in a metropolis of eight million, there had to be someone.

Then, the light bulb went off. The Wish Maker.

Duh.

At home, I'd frequently utilized her services in finding me the kind of date I was looking for. She'd make certain all my parameters were met. Of course, working with the mysterious Wish Maker came at a premium cost. Truthfully, it cost a fucking arm and a leg. But she proved worth it, every single time. I hadn't been disappointed by any of her employees yet.

"Keller," my manager Lars Gustav barked out from behind me, and I nearly jumped. Nearly. "Here late again, I see."

"Yes, sir."

"You've been making some pretty impressive strides since you arrived. Don't think I didn't notice."

I tried to disguise my inner glee. I'd hoped for some recognition while at Liddell Industries back home, but had never once been acknowledged. It was like I was invisible or something. Still, I kept my reaction to a small grin. I couldn't afford to overplay my hand.

"I appreciate you saying so."

He nodded his white blond head. "Feel free to keep doing what you're doing, but at least one night a week, go home on time. If you burn your candle at both ends for too long, you'll run out of wax and wick. So save your wick. Just sayin'."

Was he making some weird-ass pun? Between wick and dick, maybe? Humor filled his tanned Scandinavian features. I laughed, and then he was gone.

I had tons of work to do this week, but I should be able to let off the accelerator a little next week. I went back to my desk, putting out any fires. Once satisfied, I texted the mature woman known for making wishes come true.

Moved to Manhattan. Do your services still apply here? I sent.

It was only a moment before I received her message back.

Of course.

Can you have someone for me by a week from Saturday?

It'll be arranged. I'll contact you with the details.

I stretched the muscles in my back and shoulders as I took a deep breath in through my nose and blew it out through my mouth. Then, I smiled.

It felt nice to know relief was officially in sight.

3

JESSIE

As I crossed to the bulletin board outside Professor Shirley's office, I felt like I'd swallowed a boulder. The midterm scores were in, and since this one counted for ten percent of my overall grade, I needed for it to come back as at least an eighty percent or higher. I did the best I could, but since I had such a rough freshman year, I'd had to work constantly to repair my damaged GPA. Every piece of homework, every project, and every test accounted for so much.

I chewed on my inner cheek, nervous. *Please, please, please ...*

There was a scrum as classmates scrambled to see how they did, but I stood my ground. And finally, I zeroed in on my student number. I received a score of ninety-two percent. *Yes! An A!*

Thrilled and frankly a bit dazed, I wandered off to my next class. My final semester would be all about student teaching. I'd be in an actual classroom, with children ready to learn what I taught them. Like little sponges, they'd absorb some of their more significant and fundamental motor and language skills.

I couldn't wait.

We had half a semester before winter break. Before finals. Suddenly, nervousness clutched my stomach tightly again. It felt like one of those dreams where you were attempting to get somewhere but the door kept moving farther away. So close, yet not quite in reach.

"Miss?" came a creaky-sounding voice from behind me. But I didn't pause until she spoke again. "Ms. Souza?"

"Yes?" I took in an elderly-looking woman, stumbling along with a cane. I didn't recognize her. Women in her age bracket were either professors, visitors, or non-traditional students. Which could she be?

"You don't know me, but I was wondering if I could speak to you. Do you know of somewhere more private?"

"Um, sure." I led her over to an outdoor courtyard, sheltered by the high walls of the buildings on three corners. Currently, the courtyard was abandoned. Once we were seated on a decorative concrete bench, I asked, "What's this about?"

"This is an opportunity. I specialize in providing goods and services for people—all sorts of goods and services. One of those services is companionship. Essentially, what I'm asking of you is whether you'd be interested in offering your time as a dating escort for men?"

"No way," I blurted out, appalled. Who did she think she was asking me this? Who did she think *I* was? Wait, was she one of those madams? Like a female pimp or something?

Gross.

"This could be extremely beneficial to you. Financially."

How did she know I was struggling to make bank? How could she possibly know? "I'm not a prostitute," I hissed at her, not wanting to be heard.

"I never said you were, dear. But the pay for a two-hour date would amount to five thousand dollars, even with no sex involved. A longer date would pay more. A date involving sex—consensual only is my policy—would pay a minimum of ten thousand dollars, regardless of how long the date was. And I've never had any trouble with my clients confirming whether or not any sexual activity has taken place."

My ears rang with her words. Ten thousand dollars. Ten *thousand* dollars. With that kind of money, I could pay off the rest of my college education, even if I only did it once. But I couldn't. It was so ... tawdry.

"I can assure you that you would be given any pertinent information, particularly if you agree to the date involving sex or DIS for short. DIS clients must submit to blood testing, and they must communicate their expectations. Condoms are required." She handed me a card with the words "The Wish Maker," as well as a ten-digit number emblazoned underneath. "If you decide to go forward, give me a call."

Then, though her footsteps had been so halting previously, I peeked up to find her gone.

I went to my afternoon classes feeling as if that episode in the courtyard had been some surreal Twilight Zone type of hallucination. Had I dreamed all that up? Had I been roofied? Had I accidentally allowed myself to get high?

It'd all been so strange and out of the blue.

But then, I'd finger the business card she'd given me, and I knew that meeting hadn't been some peculiar figment of my imagination. It'd been real. This woman wanted to pay me thousands of dollars to do this. And I didn't even have to do a date with sex if I didn't want to. Thousands of dollars. It just seemed so impossible. And yet the woman had been so straightforward that I couldn't really call the incident creepy.

Still, I wouldn't do it. Even without the sex, I'd be entrusting myself to the utter unknown. The old lady was unknown to me, and so would be any of the men I'd be meeting up with. Or *hooking* up with. *No. Not going there.*

After finally finishing all my classes, I went home. The cutback in my hours meant I didn't have a Zumba class tonight like I used to. It was disheartening, but what could I do?

A week later, I checked my email for my Friday payment notification as I jogged up the three flights of stairs that led to the two-bedroom apartment I shared with Ashley. It was a decent yet small place in Brooklyn, nothing like the delipidated and crime-ridden apartment complex I'd been raised in. There it was, my message from PayPal. Only once I saw the amount, my feet jammed to a stop. It was half of what I'd been getting. *Half.* How could I live on so much less?

Short answer? I couldn't.

Not only was this not enough to cover the expense of my classes, it wouldn't cover my part of the rent, either. *What the actual hell?*

Huffing and puffing, I unlocked the door and slammed it behind me.

"Whoa, you look cheesed off," Ashley commented. "What happened?"

Instead of responding, I asked her a question of my own. "Why are you home? Don't you have economics right now?"

"It was cancelled. Professor injured himself playing racquetball." She giggled, her skin turning the color of a tomato. "Sorry, it's just that the rumor mill said he pulled his groin."

Ow, was my first thought. My second thought was picturing some guy pulling on, well, *himself*, until that particular portion of his anatomy was as bent out of shape as a piece of Laffy Taffy. I snorted, and the two of us laughed like tweens for a minute. It felt good. I needed to laugh more often.

"Anyway," she said, once back to herself. "Why are you cheesed off again?"

Oh, yeah. Back to our regularly scheduled programming. "You know how I told you the CrossFit gym cut my hours?"

"Yeah."

"Well, I guess I hadn't realized just how detrimental that would be to my pay. I knew it'd go down, of course, but..."

"But?" Ashley prodded.

"But it's less than half of what it was."

"Cheese and crackers," she exclaimed.

Unlike me, Ashley grew up in a strict household that didn't believe in cursing. She didn't get offended when I cussed around her, but she never did it herself, especially not with the Lord's name in vain. So instead of using a garden variety expletive, she'd say some variation with "cheese" in it. In the case of "Jesus Christ," for example, she used the phrase "cheese and crackers" with the same emphasis. It actually sounded quite similar when I thought about it.

"I'm sorry," I told her. And I really was.

For a moment, her features pinched together, her brows scrunching in distress. I knew she was contemplating going to her mom for help with this newest monetary crisis. Yet this rankled. Ashley and I were both twenty-one. Grown women. We'd been doing our best to be independent.

Still, when we ran into trouble like this—oh, who am I kidding, when *I* ran into trouble like this—Ashley often went to her mom to ask for some additional funds to keep us afloat. I hated that.

I hated it with every fiber of my being.

Her mom, while financially sound, was not especially well off. She and Ashley had been the ones to see me at my worst, and without hesitation, they'd pitched in to help. And not only with money, either. They'd provided me with a permanent shelter, clothes, and food. They'd also provided me with unending moral support. I loved Vanessa and Ashley Winter more than anyone else on this earth.

But Vanessa had moved to California for a job opportunity a year ago. She was doing her best to make things work while Ashley and I remained across the country from her. The last thing I wanted to do was make Ashley feel obligated to go to her mom and ask to borrow some extra funds. *Again*.

For a moment, I felt like shit. One of these days, Ashley would get fed up with me and kick me out of her life for good. I'd lose the only family who cared about me, as well as my best friend in the world. The back of my eyes and nose burned at the thought. Losing the Winter women would hurt me even worse than what happened with my mom.

But then, I stuck a hand in my jacket pocket. My thumb brushed up against the thick paper of the business card that odd woman had given me a week ago, and I gasped. I didn't have to cost the Winter family any more money if I didn't want to. I had another alternative, even if thinking about what this would entail made my stomach do a queasy backflip. It would be worth it, though.

Vanessa shouldn't have to pitch in to support me anymore. Enough was enough.

I touched Ashley's arm. "Don't worry," I told her. "There's this other job I can take that'll make up for it. It'll all work out, I promise."

My friend smiled at me, her eyes brightening. "Another job? Already?"

"Yeah. I uh … heard about it recently. Think I'll give the place a call. Find out about hours and so forth."

"Where is it?"

"Not sure of the address, but it'll probably be here in the city. I need to find out the specifics."

"Okay. Sounds cool. I'm gonna go study, Jess." Ashley gave me a quick hug then padded into her room.

I watched her go. Ashley was like a sister to me, and I loved her to death. She'd given me so much, while I took over and over. It was long past time for that to stop. So, I would go through with this date thing. I could prove to myself that I no longer had to be a drain on anybody's resources but my own. I pulled out the business card and plugged the number into my phone. Then, I sent the Wish Maker a text.

I'm saying yes. What do I do next?

4

TREVOR

I straightened my silk tie and glanced around the restaurant, taking in my environment. New York, like New Orleans, was a city known for its food. Where my hometown was famous for specifics tastes like Cajun, Creole, and barbecue, the Big Apple was basically a smorgasbord for any foodie on the planet.

Other than a brief text from the Wish Maker, I didn't know much about the lady friend I'd be sharing my night with.

Look for a young woman with dark curly hair. Her name is Jessie. She'll be wearing green.

And that was it. All I knew. But I sort of liked it that way. It upped the mystique. The intrigue of the situation. What's romance without a bit of mystery?

Though the term "romance" might be a stretch. This would be a hookup. No more, no less. I needed some stress relief, and I needed it now. But I'd gone through these evenings on many, many occasions. I knew the rules, and I liked the game. Being raised a Southern boy, I also liked to behave as a gentleman.

Yes, I was paying this woman for her company. And yes, she was a sure thing. But there was no need for me to be crude or for her to feel anything but comfortable in my presence. Call me old fashioned, but I liked to wine and dine my Wish Maker dates. Was it required? No. But it was good etiquette.

I might be a dom, but I wasn't a *dick*. Or at least, I made a concerted effort not to be.

Usually, I really enjoyed spending time with the women the Wish Maker chose for me. Not enough for a repeat, but still. What bachelor in his twenties would shy away from a date with an attractive woman he could then have his way with however he wanted? I liked the guarantee of that; of knowing with certainty what would happen. The fun part was seeing *how* it all played out.

As I sat with my back to a wall, so I could spot my mystery woman with her dark curly hair and green dress, I found myself judging the eatery's interior. The name of the restaurant itself was Buddakan, and it was a high-end Asian fusion place. I'd chosen it because it got such high online reviews, but now that I was here I was somewhat overwhelmed by the décor.

Not that there was anything wrong with the décor per se, it was just a bit much for my tastes. It reminded me of something Jax's parents might've liked. The place wasn't stuffy, but it was opulent, even flamboyant. It was—how could I describe it—*flashy*. Yes. The location was split into two enormous rooms, one of which had a sparkling clean and colorful bar. But it wasn't the room with the bar that was so over-the-top. It was the room I'd been taken to.

This room was high-ceilinged—and we're talking twelve-foot, at least—with candles on every table, and I shit you not, *Beauty and the Beast*-type chandeliers overhead. Like, a line of four of those suckers with a span of about five or six feet each.

Below them was a massive golden table spread down the center of the space. The thing reminded me of something you might see in a castle, and so did the intricate designs molded into the plaster walls. The whole locale gave off a kiss-my-ring-sir-knight impression.

The good news was that I'd already perused the menu, and I couldn't see how I could go wrong. There was everything from traditional dishes of egg rolls and lo mein to sushi, dim sum, and Peking duck. The cocktail menu was extensive, too. As was their wine list.

I couldn't imagine any woman not finding something she could enjoy here.

I spared a glimpse at my watch and noticed that it was five till eight. My date should arrive any time now. I'd come early, so I knew I'd have to wait. I'd given the hostess the same description the Wish Maker had given me, and I was certain my date would also give the hostess my name since I used it to make this reservation. I felt anxious, but not in a bad way. More like in anticipation.

Then, I saw a woman who I believed must be her.

Dark, no *black* curly hair, rioting around her head like a puffy cloud, and a pale green—so pale it was almost white, in fact—dress that clung to every inch of her. And that was from the back. When she turned, my heart stuttered. My God. She was the most enchanting woman I'd ever seen.

She had rich copper skin than appeared soft as butter. Though she was petite, she had deliciously rounded hips with full breasts, and most stunning of all, light green eyes that matched her high-necked mandarin-style dress. What color was that, anyway? It wasn't emerald or lime. No. The word leapt abruptly into my brain. *Jade*. My nana had some jewelry made out of that stone. Yes, jade. Definitely.

Wow. Just... fucking *wow*.

The Wish Maker had more than earned her commission on this one.

I'd been with a lot of women. I mean, a *lot*. All of them at least hitting the spectrum somewhere near pretty. But this woman was more than pretty. She was more than beautiful. More than hot.

Damn, maybe I'd been lonelier than I'd thought.

Jesus, get it together, Keller.

The hostess was bringing her over, so I rose to my feet.

"Jessie?" I asked her, offering my hand palm up.

"Yes." She had a deeper voice than most women. Sultry. Luscious. But still distinctly feminine. She clasped my hand as if to shake it, but I turned it so I could press my lips briefly to her knuckles, instead.

"Trevor Keller."

"Nice to meet you."

Her tone came out the teeniest degree stilted, but I was too distracted by my physical reaction to her to notice. The second we'd made contact, I'd gotten hard. Not like a semi, either, but full-on hickory tree stump from my backyard at home hard.

Normally, I would've remained standing so I could pull out her chair for her, but due to my visibly observable condition, I didn't this time. I slammed down into my chair with enough force to almost topple the stupid thing, then lamely kicked at the feet of *her* chair so it would scoot backwards across the carpeted floor.

Smooth move, asshole.

She stared at the jerky movement of her chair, then sliding a hand over the back of her dress, sat with far more grace than I'd shown. Okay, so I hadn't been this awkward on a date in years, particularly not a Wish Maker date. But I would recover. Still, it was difficult to think of things I could do that would be suave or charming when all the blood was missing from my brain.

"So, your name is Jessie?" I asked her, and she narrowed her gaze at me as if I had two heads. The fact that my lower head was attempting to swell its way out of my pants like a fucking gopher wasn't exactly helping me think on my feet here.

"Yes. Is there something wrong with the name Jessie?"

Her tone was challenging. Not the best of signs.

The thing was that "Jessie" did not suit her. Not even a little. She was so enticing and magnetic. A better name for her would've been something like Francesca or Alexandria. "Jessie" reminded me of some pioneer woman who lived a tough existence on the frontier or something. Someone who could shoot a shotgun at a marauding bear or pack of wolves. "Jessie" was not this seductive temptress presently sitting in front of me.

"No," I answered quickly. "Of course not. It's just …" Why was I fumbling around like fifteen-year-old? I was customarily an excellent communicator, I *swear*. "You're so captivating. And while the name Jessie is fine, it strikes me as too plain for you."

I hoped she'd take this as the compliment I'd meant it to be rather than an insult. For a moment, I watched her, unsure. Fortunately, our server appeared. Since I'd given my date zero time to check out the menu, we weren't anywhere near ready to order. But I did manage to score us a pot of tea, a couple of waters, as well as a cup of Saki for each of us. Christ knew I needed something to take the edge off.

In the few minutes that passed after that, my date studied the expansive menu. As soon as our drinks arrived, I downed the Saki and asked for another.

There, that was better.

"I've never had Saki before," Jessie said, though she kept her eyes on the list of foods in her hands. She then took a sip, blinking as if it'd burnt her. "God, it's strong."

"It is," I agreed. "Let me pour you some tea." I took the pot and filled her delicate teacup to the brim. She sipped some, then drank more.

"This is better."

"Have whatever you want," I told her.

We ordered a tasting menu, which meant we'd receive a varied selection, then waited for the dishes in silence. I'd had two Sakis but still felt like I was floundering. I'd never felt so out of my element in my life. The only saving grace was that my arousal had diminished with every tense moment we suffered through.

I needed to get the conversation moving again, that was all.

Once the dishes came, it gave me an idea. We'd been given a dozen items to fill our table, almost like our own private buffet.

"How familiar are you with these sorts of foods?" I asked her.

"I've had Chinese, of course. Stuff like chow mein and chop suey, but I've never tried some of these."

Yes. Awesome. "Then may I ask you a favor? Can I fill your plate for you? I'm quite good at choosing, and if you don't enjoy my selections, I'll keep trying till I find something that you'll love."

She smirked at me, as if doubting my ability, and I smirked back. Things hadn't been going easily between us so far, and I wanted to win her over, even if she'd been hired to please me instead of the other way around. I wondered if this was her first Wish Maker date but didn't ask. It didn't matter because as bumpy as things had been tonight, I loved a good challenge.

I loaded her plate and set it before her. She liked four of the five items she tasted on the first go-around, which gave me confidence to choose again for her. She nibbled and tasted the second round, this time liking every bit of it.

"This is fun," she declared, brushing the corner of her ridiculously plump rosebud lips with the corner of her napkin.

"Glad you're enjoying yourself."

"Jessica Isabelle Souza," she said, tossing me a close-lipped grin, and I raised an eyebrow at her. "That's my legal name. I've always gone by Jessie, though. Ever since I can remember."

She took a drink of the flowery tea, and once she set her cup down, I captured her hand. Turning her wrist so the underside was exposed, I kissed my way across the tender skin. She shivered noticeably. So, I licked a trail along the same path, blowing on it gently as I stared into her jade green eyes.

"Thank you for sharing. *Jessica* makes much more sense," I whispered, and this time she shuddered even more obviously as she let those eyes of hers drift shut in pleasure.

My body jumped to attention again so fast that I felt lightheaded, but I did my best not to show it, offering her a slow grin instead. Christ, I wanted her. And now that our dinner was complete, I would have her.

"You ready to go?" I asked her as a courtesy, and she nodded.

"Yes, I believe so."

I took her to a five-star hotel. I never dallied with women in my home; I liked to keep my sex life and my home life separate. Still, Jessica was everything I'd hoped she'd be. Passionate. Wild. Willing to submit. She was a dream between the sheets. In fact, she was so good that I left her asleep in the bed the following morning so she could wake up at her leisure.

Jessica almost made me decide to break with my own stringent policy of never seeing any of these women again. She'd been amazing in more ways than one. But that's simply not how I rolled. Something told me that if I went back for seconds with her, that I'd be back for thirds. And if I went back after that, I'd be in big trouble. If she was this difficult to walk away from now, how could I do it after experiencing more of her?

Better to be safe than sorry. I didn't have time for a relationship, and clearly, since she was working as an escort for the Wish Maker, neither did she. It'd be best to go our own separate ways.

Still, as I descended the stairs toward the lobby of the hotel, I felt tempted to go back. It was as if she was pulling me back to her. I even paused mid-step, thinking about it. But, no. I'd come to this city to jumpstart my career, not get involved with someone. That's why I'd hired the Wish Maker to begin with. I didn't need any romantic entanglements, no matter how awesome the sex was. I had to keep forging my way forward and building on my dream.

So I kept going, even though as my taxi drove me across town, I kept searching for the hotel among the others along the skyline. I felt this bizarre sensation in my chest I couldn't identify. A hollowness I didn't know how to explain.

I watched as the hotel vanished behind other taller structures, unable to keep myself from looking back.

5

JESSIE

When I woke, I sat up with a start, disoriented by my alien surroundings. For a moment, terror seized my breath. Then, like one of those games where the images go from blurred to clear, my memories from the previous night emerged.

Meeting my date in that extravagant restaurant. The tension that had stayed between us like a roadblock in the beginning. How things had eased over time with the help of some powerful Japanese alcohol. How the tension evolved into something teasing and light. How he'd touched me, exciting me with an intensity and sensuality I'd never experienced before.

How we'd had multiple bouts of sex until the wee hours of the morning.

I thought of what Ashley might say about this if I ever were to tell her and knew instantly. Her soprano voice crying, *"Cheese and crackers,"* reverberated against my skull, making me snicker to myself.

Cheese and crackers, for sure.

The silken softness of the luxurious two thousand count sheet set shifted against my bare skin, and I sighed. I'd never in my life enjoyed such eroticism or pure ecstasy. I'd become lost to it; to all the things Trevor did to me. I'd been so frighteningly nervous when I'd ambled into that restaurant, and when we hadn't connected right off the bat, I'd seriously considered fleeing the scene.

I told myself that maybe this was a mistake, and that I shouldn't do it. I almost ran. But then, something remarkable had happened. Whatever weirdness had plagued us evaporated like mist in the sun, and we'd become drawn together like magnets flipped to the correct side. By the time we'd finished dinner, I'd been so turned on that I feared that my pebbled nipples might show through both my bra and my dress. My breasts had become so heavy that they ached.

Quite literally.

And that hadn't been the only part of me to ache, either.

I rubbed the sleep from my eyes and then twisted in the bed. My hand brushed against something that crinkled beneath me. It was a sheet of paper from the hotel stationery. A note.

Jessica,

Last night was incredible. Check out isn't until noon, so feel free to take your time. Order a room service breakfast on me, if you'd like. I'm sorry I had to dash off before you woke, but it's always better this way.

Thank you for an extremely pleasurable evening,

Trevor

I pitched forward so that my head plunged into his pillow. It smelled like him. Like musk, and somehow, rain. I breathed him in, allowing myself to memorize his scent, even though it was unlikely we'd ever cross paths again in the future. His note made that clear. Which was good. That's what I wanted, too. The last thing I had time for in my life was a man.

Even one as scrumptious as Trevor Keller.

I still remembered how he'd looked as he stood for me in Buddakan. While nearly everyone I knew was taller than me, he'd towered over me by a good foot. Still, he hadn't come across as intimidating. He'd had light brown hair cut in a simple masculine style. An expensive pinstriped suit in charcoal gray with a matching tie. A carefully trimmed goatee that framed one of the most arousing smiles I've ever seen on a guy.

But what got to me the most had been his eyes. They'd been deep set but expressive and playful. They'd also been brown, not the dark brown I typically saw, but this lighter, richer color. They'd had this unusual metallic sheen to them, a reflective quality like gold.

They reminded me of the piece of amber Ashley had in her room. She was studying archaeology and had had that amber —with the mosquito trapped inside just like in Jurassic Park —since she was four. I'd never seen anyone with eyes like his. And I'd been sorely tempted to grab his face and study their depths all night.

Which would've been ridiculous.

Still, as much as I questioned spending a night with a man for money, I felt okay with it. Trevor had been, hands down, the best lover ever. Somehow, he seemed to sense what I needed, then he'd fulfill that need. I hadn't expected to receive any pleasure myself last night. I knew what I was there to do, and that it was his orgasms that were important. Yet, he'd gone out of his way to make sure I received just as many climaxes as he had.

Hell, if we were to measure how many times I'd come in numbers, then I received *more*.

God.

Even now, hours later, my body still thrummed with it all.

I climbed out of the bed, still naked, and hopped in the massive shower. Trevor had spared no expense on anything, that was for sure. I thought about ordering room service like he'd suggested but decided against it. I had a semester and a half of school left so I might as well hunker down and prepare for it.

As I soaped and shampooed up, I thought about another instance when I scrubbed my body after a sexual encounter. I half expected to feel as dirty now as I had then, but I didn't. What I'd experienced with Trevor had felt wonderful, not upsetting or wrong. And even though it'd crossed some lines for me, it hadn't hurt. There had been no pain.

I scrutinized my body once I toweled off, looking for any evidence of what he'd done to me. There were no scuff marks around my wrists or ankles. No hickeys. No bruising of any kind. He'd gone from soft touches to something much rougher, but at no point had I freaked out or felt unsafe. He'd checked in on me constantly, which I found surprisingly sweet.

Not to mention so scorching hot I was shocked we didn't melt the damn mattress.

As I padded from the bathroom to the bed, I saw no evidence of what accoutrement he'd used on me. But I did spot something on the floor. It was a receipt, the kind you might see on an online delivery order. I glanced at the paper. The order had been for two days before, and it'd been for a super supreme pizza with pineapple, eight wings, and a two liter of Dr. Pepper.

I smiled. This felt like an unexpected peek into Trevor's life. When he wasn't hiring escorts and banging them against the headboard of a fancy hotel four-poster or going to five-star restaurants, he apparently liked to kick back at his place with some pizza and wings. I liked the normalcy of that.

The man had been such a dichotomy. Gentle and tender yet dominating. Generous and kind, yet also awkward. This receipt amounted to one more clue about this beautiful rich man who apparently preferred to pay for dates rather than simply ask a woman out.

Which was, frankly, weird as hell.

But, whatever. I tucked the slip of paper into my purse. I didn't know why. It wasn't like I'd probably ever see him again.

Still.

Ready to get a move on now, I threw on my mandarin dress again. Ashley's mom had purchased it for me one Christmas, but I hadn't had a fancy enough event to wear it to until last night. Almost everything else I owned was of the denim, yoga or workout variety.

Straightening my clothing, I made sure I wasn't forgetting anything. I scanned the room, letting my memories fill me one last time, then I allowed the door to lock itself behind me. I was in such a good mood until I reached the door of my apartment. I changed clothes and settled in to study, but then, I hadn't been able to concentrate. I kept thinking about Trevor. About the way he'd made me feel. How he'd played my body like a well-tuned violin.

And now, I felt the absence of him like a pang.

I kept going back to my books over and over, but no matter what, my mind still wandered to that hotel bed. Maybe it was the thoughtfulness of his actions with me that were the culprit. I hadn't anticipated that. I'd believed he'd give me nothing but raunchy, hard, nasty sex, but he hadn't. He'd been so careful with me, and even when he'd engaged *full engines,* so to speak, he'd still asked me if I was okay.

But I had to be real. He'd been my client, that's all. I'd given him what he'd paid me for, and then, he'd left before we'd have to say any unsettling goodbyes. Which was smart of him. Tactful. Considerate.

So why couldn't I stop thinking of him?

I rubbed my hands over my face, frustrated at my lack of concentration. I went to the sink and splashed icy cold water on my face, then I made myself some dark roast coffee. I was worn out—for obvious reasons—but I'd been tired before. Wrapping up my chaotic hair, I took a few gulps of my coffee and went back to my notes.

I returned to an old technique I knew would work. I yanked out my phone and started a voice memo, reading my notes out loud. Doing this always helped me push through, and since Ashley wasn't here, I wouldn't even disturb her. Feeling satisfaction at my solution—as well as from other things—I read on, committing my work to memory.

6

TREVOR

"We've had the best fiscal quarter all year, and in celebration, I'm informing each of you of your increased individual bonuses," Lars said, as an intern passed out envelopes.

I opened mine, shocked at the number of zeros I saw. I glimpsed around at my other colleagues. Most of them seemed pleased, a few even wearing expressions I'd have to call smug. Many were grinning to themselves, possibly imagining what they might spend their new increased budget on. For my part, I felt happy, but knew I had to keep going. This bonus helped to make me a multi-millionaire—which was great—but I still wanted that golden ring.

I wanted what my best friend had. I wanted to be a *billionaire*.

My supervisor began to move on to world interests in the financial market, and I listened with half an ear until I heard him say, "The Deutsche Bank surrendered to Wall Street a few months ago, and our goal is to make sure that all European banks follow suit."

Surrender. The word ricocheted through my psyche. I'd said that word to Jessica a few nights ago. Or a week ago now. Shit, had it already been a week?

"Surrender to me, and I'll make this *so* good for you," I'd whispered into her ear. Her black curls had been tickling my face as I'd said them, and for whatever reason, those sweet-smelling strands had called to me like a siren.

Jessica had been one of those rare women who didn't wear perfume. Her scent had been light, natural, and barely there. Yet, I'd tasted it on every inch of her skin. She'd smelled tantalizing, like honey. How did she do that? Was it a soap she used? A bodywash? Some sort of edible lotion?

"Okay, that's all I have. Does anyone have questions about anything I've gone over this morning?" Lars asked, and I blinked. I'd missed the tail end of this meeting because I'd been preoccupied about my night with Jessica.

Again.

Goddammit. This was getting to be a problem.

"Keller, you all right?" my manager asked me, his eyes boring into my forehead.

"Yes, sir. Sure."

"Good, because we have an important merger coming up, and I'm thinking about letting you take the lead on it." He cracked a smile.

"Seriously?"

"Yeah," he said, putting up a fist for me to bump. I did.

I hadn't even been with the bank a year. This was a gigantic gesture of trust of his part, and I couldn't let him down. "I'm honored, sir. Truly."

"I know I warned you about burning the candle at both ends, but that's precisely what taking the lead on this will require. It'll mean long hours and working right through the upcoming holidays," he told me, his face growing more hesitant, as if expecting me to back peddle. "That going to be an issue?"

"Absolutely not," I said, undeniably aware of the fact that I was being a kiss-ass and hoping it didn't come across that way to my manager. But what was worse was what I hadn't said.

I live to serve. That quip had been on my lips, and I'd nearly said it aloud. I had to learn how to stifle my smartass remarks so I could make a good impression in this job, but the sarcasm remained there just beneath the surface. I wondered if I'd ever grow in prominence enough with the firm to be able to unleash it without consequence.

Taking the lead on this might be the first in a series of steps to make that a reality. I had to do it.

So I would.

My cell phone buzzed in my pocket, and I glanced at the time. Eleven o'clock at night. It was late to be at the office, even for me. But over the past week, I'd worked fourteen-hour days to prepare for the upcoming merger. It would take place right after the new year, and I didn't want to fail. Couldn't afford to.

So here I was in the office with my best friend's number lighting up my screen. I considered not taking it. What kind of friend makes a social call at this hour? But then, I realized in his time zone, it was only ten. Late enough to be home without being in bed. So, rather than decline the call, I hit "accept."

"Hey, Jax."

"What's the good word, Trevor?" my best friend asked into the phone, sounding cheerful.

It was still a bit odd to hear him sound so upbeat, for four years he'd sounded clinically depressed every time I spoke to him. But that was all over now.

Instead of answering his question, I hit him with one of my own. "How's married life treating you?"

"It's awesome. And Alec is starting to pull up on furniture now. I think he'll be walking pretty soon."

Alec, Jax's son, had been born nine months prior. My best friend had been thrilled to be present at the birth. Their first baby, a daughter named Callie, had been born unbeknownst to him, so holding his wife Roxy's hand while encouraging her to push had been tremendously significant to him. I still remember showing up with blue balloons to the hospital, only to step inside the room and see him gazing at his son in awe, tears running down his cheeks.

In years past, I would've raked him over the coals for such a thing. But that time, after having seen what he and his wife had been through, I didn't have the heart to yank his chain. It didn't mean I wouldn't give him shit for other stuff, though.

"You two still fucking on the couch at every available opportunity?" I had a huge smile on my face as I said this. I'd stopped over to bring something by once, and they'd forgotten I was coming. So instead, I got to see *them* come. Both of them, right before my eyes.

"Man, uncool. I really wish you'd let that go. And don't you dare mention it in front of Roxy when you get here. She still hides her face every time you mention it."

I knew that. I *enjoyed* that. Yet, his mention of my upcoming visit reminded me of what I hadn't gotten around to telling him.

"Hey, look, Jax. I'm sorry to tell you this, but I'm not going to make it for Christmas this year after all."

"What?" he sounded indignant. "But we've been planning on you being here. Callie and Alec are growing like weeds, and you're missing it."

I knew that. I was missing a lot of things. But staying here couldn't be helped. Although part of me felt disappointed, another part—a part I actively hid from Jax and Roxy both— felt relieved that I wouldn't now have to be around all that blissed-out lovey dovey stuff for forty-eight hours straight.

"I know, and I'm sorry. But this opportunity came up at work, and it's a big deal, you know? I need to do it. I'm still a junior executive and need to prove myself however I can."

There was a lengthy pause. "I get it," he told me, but truthfully, I didn't think he did. "Just get back here when you can, okay? New York might as well be as far away as London at this point."

Fuck. Guilt trip, much? He probably didn't mean it that way, but comparing his old situation—which hadn't been his choice—to mine as if they were the same, sucked balls. I wasn't going to call him on it, though. Not when I was already letting him down.

"Listen, man, I gotta go."

"Yeah, okay. Take care of yourself, Trev. And happy holidays."

"You, too," I said, then disconnected.

Today, I'd come into the office at six in the morning, and it was now after eleven. A seventeen-hour day was a new record for me, but I doubted it would be the last. Planting the heels of my hands over my eye sockets, I rested them until my vision went cool and black, then wiped away the grit.

I stood, realized I was too fucking tired to drive, and clicked on my Uber app. It was time to head home.

∼

I'd been too out of it to stand in the shower, so I'd brushed my teeth, dropped trou', and fell listlessly into my bed.

Then, I was galloping like a horse around the pristine tile and stainless steel of my kitchen. Like, actually pretending to ride a horse with the reins and everything. A child was holding onto my head, its legs on either side of my neck, whooping and hollering out, "Giddyap! Giddyap!"

I saw our reflection in the reflective surface of my backsplash and recognized the child. It was Callie, Jax's daughter. "Faster," she yelled then, squealing when dream me picked up the pace. "Faster, Daddy."

Daddy?

And then I realized, here in this dream, fantasy, alternate reality, or whatever it was, I had somehow filled Jax's shoes. A woman laughed, and I turned, thinking I'd see Roxy behind me, but it wasn't my best friend's wife at all. It was Jessie Souza.

Jessica.

She approached me with a wide smile and so much love in those jade eyes of hers that I nearly burst. Her skin, a few shades darker than mine, made a breathtaking contrast against my hand as she reached out to me, lacing our fingers together. She was beautiful, and Callie was beautiful, and even I was beautiful as we all stood there contentedly next to my colossal fridge.

The next thing I knew, my alarm clock was blaring at me. I slapped at it, nearly flinging it across my bedroom. Discombobulated, I sat there on my mattress, scowling hard enough that the skin of my face felt twisted too tight. As I slowly absorbed that my idyllic little scene had no basis whatsoever in reality, I felt myself come fully awake.

More alert now and twice as grumpy, I thrust out from beneath my bed linens. My windows—expensive floor-to-ceiling numbers—remained dark, which meant dawn had not yet broken. I was able to see the famous Manhattan skyline, though, with the Chrysler building, Empire State, and the Freedom Tower gleaming in the background.

That's why I'd agreed to rent this apartment. While it was no penthouse, it did overlook Central Park and was high enough to garner some fantastic views.

It cost a pretty penny, but I enjoyed the prestige of it being mine. Living here helped me to feel like Jax wasn't outdoing me. Here, I could feel like his equal. Like I was just as capable as he was of having a successful life.

And maybe, just maybe, when the requirements of my job settled into something easier to handle, I could quit trying to prove myself. I could stop relying on the Wish Maker to provide me with dates. Instead, I could focus on discovering a woman who would see all that I had to offer and decide that despite my quirks and sexual depravity, I was worth being with.

That I was worthy of their love.

7

JESSIE

JANUARY

At eight that night, I had to drag myself up the three flights of stairs to our apartment through sheer force of will. I was just so goddamn exhausted all the time. Between student teaching five days a week, my Zumba class, and taking on a handful of personal training clients, I was dead beat at the end of each day.

My hands shaking, I unlocked the door and pushed myself to our loveseat. Ashley appeared from inside our kitchen.

"Hello, sunshine," she called out, but then getting a good look at me, hurried over. She laid her palm on my forehead as if checking for a temperature. "You're all clammy, and you've got dark circles under your eyes. Are you sick?"

For the past week, our school and work schedules had overlapped, so we'd only caught glimpses of one another on our way in or out.

"Nuh-uh," I said, shaking my head. "Just wiped."

While the money from my Wish Maker date had helped a great deal, I'd decided doing it more than once was out of the question. I'd done it because I'd had to, and I'd experienced lots of nights that were worse. But right now, I could tell myself it'd been a fluke. A one-time aberration. If I did it again, I'd have to call having sex for money what it was, and I didn't ever want to do that.

Ashley dumped some Ragu into a bowl and put it in the microwave as she boiled some spaghetti noodles on one of the two burners on our stovetop. Within moments, the smell of tomato sauce filled the room, and I groaned with longing.

"Hungry?" my BFF asked me.

I grunted at her and she snickered, a pasta spoon in her hand.

"You remind me of my aunt when she was pregnant with Carson." Carson was Ashley's baby cousin. Her aunt had been going through menopause and had thought her lack of menstruation meant she was no longer fertile. Turned out, she still was. "You do, though. I hear you getting up all hours of the night, and then you're sluggish during the day. You're hungry, grouchy, and not yourself."

Fatigued as I was, my bladder chose that instant to not just become full, but to do so urgently. "Shit," I mumbled, as I stumbled into the bathroom.

"That's another thing," my friend shouted through the door, which was completely unnecessary. The door was paper thin. "You're going pee more, too."

"Maybe it's an infection," I said without raising my voice. I wondered how bad it would be if I fell asleep on the pot.

"Then maybe you should go to the doctor."

"I hate doctors." I did, too. Well, hate is a strong word. But after the worst night of my life, which had subsequently led to me drifting around like a vagabond, I had to go to a free clinic. One of the doctors there apparently resented having to give away his time without getting paid, because he treated me with about as much warmth as a bedpan that had been stuck in the freezer.

"I'm serious, sweetie."

I came back out. "Yeah, me, too."

"Here," she said, sprinkling Dollar Tree parmesan, that wasn't really parmesan, on the top of our full plates. "Maybe this'll make you feel better."

I ate, took a very short shower, then slept. And then, as per usual lately, I turned over in my twin bed and couldn't fall back asleep. It had been like this for a while, and I didn't know why. I'd been a bit stressed out, but I'd never suffered insomnia this severe before. Needing to go to the bathroom again, I headed in there and took a gander at my cotton panties.

It occurred to me that I didn't remember the last time I had a period. But irregular periods were normal for me. I'd have one two weeks apart, then skip for months at a time. The longest spread had lasted for four months. This time, I hadn't had one in three. Oh, well.

I laid flat on my back and peered up at our rather dingy ceiling. That dinginess was our fault. Ashley and I both loved to burn candles, and the smoke made the ceiling and walls all sooty.

Still, I didn't want to give up the practice. I loved the smell of them too much.

I focused on a spot that looked darker than the rest, my mind rewinding to the conversation I'd had with Ashley. She'd been so silly, comparing me to her aunt. It almost sounded like she thought I might be knocked up or something. I wasn't. What a crazy idea. I'd only had sex once in the past year, and that'd been a desperate one-off to help pay for college and rent.

Granted, it'd been a very good one-off. Fabulous, even.

My body had buzzed for days after that. In the best possible way.

But we'd used protection. Well, I assumed we did. I hadn't been able to visually verify anything since I'd been blindfolded at the time. All four of those times.

Surely, Trevor had been responsible, though. Right?

I bolted up into a seated position, suddenly feeling a little too awake. Throwing on some clothes and slip-on shoes, I tossed my wallet and keys into my pocket and skittered down the block to the twenty-four-hour pharmacy. It was just after three in the morning, but I needed to confirm that I wasn't…

No. I couldn't even allow myself to think it.

I bought a couple of stick tests and raced back home, holing up in the bathroom. For a long minute, I held the bright pink box in my hands, feeling afraid. But I hadn't come this far to back down now. It was time to woman up, put my big girl panties on, and discover the truth.

Whatever that was.

Following the directions to the letter, I took the first one. Then I took the other right afterwards. It felt like if I just did this quickly, everything would be all right. Both came back with the same result. After that, I sort of slid off the closed toilet to crumple like a twisted pretzel onto the floor by the pedestal sink. I couldn't accept what I'd seen, even though I was still staring at it this very minute.

I squinted down at the two unmistakable pink lines and had to put my head between my knees.

The sound of rushing water filled my ears, and I had no idea if the noise was real or coming from inside my own head. My body felt hot, then cold, then hot again, before every one of my limbs seemed to go totally numb except for my fingers, which were tingling.

I closed my eyes and pressed my temple against the porcelain of the sink. I needed to ground myself somehow because it felt as if I'd been jettisoned out an airlock and into outer space.

I lived in a postage stamp-sized apartment and paid less rent than my roommate, which I could still barely afford. I was single and so close to obtaining my bachelor's degree that I could taste it. I was living with my best friend, dependent on my part-time jobs, and often had to scrimp and save just to help Ashley make our ends meet.

And despite the fact that I felt like my life was hanging by the thinnest of threads, my two over-the-counter tests had both come back positive.

I was pregnant.

8

TREVOR

I greeted the end of another long day with my feet up in my recliner, a craft beer, and a football game on my big screen. It'd been one of those days where everything had been like pulling teeth. I kept playing phone tag with not one but three of my clients. Lars was on vacation which meant I had to cover both his workload and my own. And on top of everything else, both the Dow Jones and NASDAQ index had tanked across the board.

Not Great Depression or 2008 recession tanked, but it'd gone down steeply. My clients had lost money and so had I. Not that I was all that worried over the long term. To be a good investor, you had to see these sorts of dips in the market as a matter of doing business, and I did. Yet it still sucked because getting screamed at or consoling clients for hours and hours straight did not a fun day make.

But hey, it was a living.

I did my best to lose myself in the game on the screen. My Saints were playing the 49ers, and I always rooted for my home team. I had since I was a toddler. Some of my happier memories involved sitting with my dad and watching those gold helmets with our beloved fleur-de-lis throw that pigskin across the field.

It also helped me to feel a little less homesick.

The Saints had just taken the lead when a knock issued from my door. I contemplated ignoring that knock. Although I'd had a busy social life back in New Orleans, here I'd made no real friends. I didn't go out to bars with my coworkers, so I hadn't really bonded with any of them. Lars had invited me to go out once or twice, but since I'd felt the need to stay in the office working later than him, I'd always begged off.

So, since I had no social life and hadn't asked for any food to be delivered on this particular night, I had no idea who might be on the other side of my door.

The knock came again, louder and more urgent this time, so with a groan of reluctance, I hauled my ass out of my extremely comfy seat to go answer it. I peered through the peephole, but all I could see was a shapely-looking shadow, as if a woman was standing off to the side. Bemused, I eased open my door to find a surprise.

Jessie Souza. Although I continued to think of her as Jessica. I called her by that name repeatedly during the night we'd spent together.

And she'd *liked* it. If her screams of rapturous delight were any indication, anyway.

I hadn't seen her in months. At least three months, in fact. She was still astonishingly appealing to me. But then, it occurred to me that I hadn't told her where I lived. How the hell had she found my private residence?

"I need to speak with you," she said, barreling in past me.

"By all means, I guess," I answered, struggling to bite back my sarcasm. I didn't want to be rude to her, but she'd barged in on me uninvited without any warning at all. I started to close my door, but then merely pushed it to. She wouldn't be staying. I'd make sure of it.

"Listen …" she began, but then paused, her mouth opening and shutting several times. For the first time I noticed that her mannerisms were off. She seemed jittery, as if she'd had way too much coffee. Yet her eyes had dark semi-circles underneath them as if she hadn't slept.

While I couldn't help being annoyed—I maintained a stringent rule to never *ever* re-establish contact with any of my former Wish Maker dates—her peculiar behavior did cause me to feel a flicker of concern. "Are you all right?"

"I'm ... pregnant."

I blinked at her, stunned. "Congratulations?" I said cautiously, my words coming out as more of an inquiry than anything else. Why had she tracked me down to tell me this? There was no possibility that I had anything to do with her ... condition. I went out of my way to avoid such eventualities.

"You're the father."

"I most certainly am not," I spat out at her, irritated now. Not once had I had sex without a condom. Never, ever. I'd always been extremely disciplined in that regard. My bedroom habits might be kinky, but that didn't mean I wasn't careful. If anything, my preferences made me even *more* careful. "And I don't appreciate you popping in here unannounced and casting such an accusation at me."

My entire day had been a shitshow, and now this.

"I ..." She seemed shocked that I'd deny it. But I wasn't about to fall prey to some gold digger scam. "You *are*. This isn't something I would lie about."

I huffed out a humorless laugh, smirking openly at her now. Whatever her game was, I wasn't playing it. "Yeah, I'm sorry you found yourself in such a predicament, but I had nothing to do with it."

I figured she'd back down at that. My tone had been not only sarcastic but cutting. Yet she squared her shoulders and stood her ground. "You're the only one I've been with in the past *year*, Trevor."

Did she honestly expect me to believe that? Jessie Souza was one of the sexiest creatures I'd ever met. Men probably hit on her on a daily basis. Once they picked their jaws up off the ground, anyway. So her claiming that I had been her only recent lover had to be bullshit. *There's no way. Just, no fucking way.*

Still, I'd better unearth what she was really after so I could be prepared. My irritation escalated into real anger. I'd misjudged her. She'd come across as sweet, maybe even a little naïve. But clearly, that'd been an act. Not only had she inextricably managed to track my ass down, she was aiming lies at me like a javelin. Mean lies. So, she was either a creepy stalker or a con artist or both.

"Let's just cut to the chase here, shall we?" I suggested, the words themselves might've been polite but my tone was pure ice. "Why don't you tell me why you went to all this trouble to seek me out? Exactly how much do you want?"

"How much?" she spluttered out.

Oh, come on.

"Christ, if you really want me to spell it out for you, I will. *Money*. How much money are you after? What's the magic number that'll make certain you never darken my doorstep again?" Not than I planned on giving her any.

Dammit, this had never happened to me before. I supposed I'd have to go to the Wish Maker and lodge a complaint. The whole point in going to her in the first place was to avoid crap like this. She should've vetted this Jessie Souza better, if Jessie Souza or Jessica Isabelle weren't just made-up aliases.

"I don't want your money," she squeaked out. Seriously, the girl actually squeaked. Maybe she hoped the sad sound would make her more sympathetic or something. "I ... I just wanted to inform you."

Right.

"So that ... what?" I asked her. She hadn't sought me out for nothing. I didn't believe that for a second.

"So that you would know." She touched her abdomen when she said it, and my gaze followed her movement.

If this woman really was preggers, wouldn't it be more noticeable? Shouldn't she be more rounded out? I'd seen Jax's wife Roxy as her pregnancy progressed, and her body had changed dramatically. Even early on, if you looked at Roxy pointedly enough, you could tell she had a baby on the way. I stared at Jessie Souza's tiny waist. It looked as flat and tight as I remembered it from a few months ago.

Other than appearing more bedraggled than she'd been the night of our date, I saw no other discernible difference in her. *So go sell your wares to some other sap, darlin'.*

"Well, you told me." I put finger quotes up in the air when saying the word "told." How dare she try to pull a fast one on me. I'd really liked her, too. Unlike most of my Wish Maker dates, Jessica had made frequent reappearances in my warm shower time performances. She'd been *so* hot. And now, she'd ruined my image of her completely. I yanked my door open and waved her toward it. "Time for you to go. Bye now."

Jesus, I hoped she wasn't crazy, like legitimately so. I'd hate to have to deal with that on top of everything else.

I squinted at her warily, and that's when I saw it. Tears glimmering in her eyes unshed. Damn, she was good. Seeing that actually made me feel bad. Guilty. Because if she was to turn out pregnant for real, that would make me a total douche. Then, as quickly as the emotion went on display, she sniffled and steeled her petite spine. I was struck by the difference in our heights again. She was such a little wisp of a thing. But she had balls, I had to give her that.

Those almost tears nearly tripped me up. Nice touch.

Without another word, she stormed through my door and out into the hallway, heading for the elevator. I wondered if I hadn't already had a hold of the door, if she would've slammed it. That would've made a strong impression, right? Added to the melodrama of her fake situation.

I went back to my recliner, trying to return to my game, but though I watched the screen, my mind was elsewhere. Not in a million years would I ever have anticipated getting accused of such a thing.

I shook my head at myself. See, this was why I didn't date in the traditional way. I didn't need this in my life. This stress and uneasiness. Even though she was the guilty party, I still felt yucky now. Being kind and gentlemanly to the opposite sex had been engrained in me since birth, but I hadn't acted like that tonight. Not that she'd deserved being treated nicely, but still.

Ugh. I was damned either way.

The longer I sit there blocking out the football game, the longer doubts began to creep into my brain. Doubts and questions. How did she locate me? Why did she target me? And worst of all, why hadn't she asked anything of me?

That was the thing that made the least sense of all. Why come here, disrupt my night, accuse me of impregnating me, and then just leave with nothing? Was it because I called her bluff? She hadn't asked for money. She hadn't asked for a ring. She hadn't even asked for my time beyond the few minutes it'd taken her to weave her tale of woe.

I downed the rest of my beer in a few gulps, then leapt up to get something stronger. Beer wasn't going to do it tonight. I knocked back a few shots of whiskey, not stopping until the room around me looked fuzzy around the edges. I felt warmer and more relaxed now, so I threw back one additional shot before sauntering back to my recliner and falling into it. Putting my feet up, I let the images from my television float blearily by. My eyes felt heavy.

When I felt myself nodding off, I was glad.

What I needed more than anything from this day was for it to end.

9

JESSIE

For the following two days I stayed in bed, vacillating between misery and near hysteria. The whole scenario was a bit too familiar to me. I hadn't ever thought I'd wind up back in such a similar place again.

I didn't know what I'd hoped for when I'd gone to Trevor's posh Manhattan apartment. But I hadn't foreseen his reaction at all. He'd denied it flat out, had acted as if I was a liar. Then, when he'd accused me of trying to get money out of him, my brain had sort of gone offline. It was the last thing I'd thought he'd say.

I thought maybe he'd tell me what he wanted. Whether he thought it'd be a good idea to go through with this or not. If I was going to get rid of it, that decision needed to be made sooner rather than later. And I wanted his opinion, either way.

Instead, I'd received snarky comments and incredulity. And ire. He'd been furious at me. Not because I was pregnant, but because he'd thought I'd planned to cheat him. Of all the twisted fucked-up notions to have. I'd been so sideswiped by this that I hadn't known how to respond. So, I'd left. And I had no intention of going back.

I played out various what-ifs in my head. What if I got rid of it? I couldn't afford a child. I was struggling terribly as it was. If I terminated the pregnancy, then that would probably be better for me. My life would go on like it had been. I'd complete my degree and hopefully find a teaching job. Everything would stay on course.

Except that my heart would break into hundreds of pieces. When I let myself go there and think about scheduling an abortion, I felt sick. Physically ill. I'd experienced a miscarriage once in my life already, and it'd been excruciating in every sense of the word. I didn't think I could *choose* to end the pregnancy, no matter how much financial sense it might make.

I wanted to be responsible and make the most logical decision, but I had to allow for more than logic, as well. If I let things progress naturally, that group of cells inside of me would change and grow. With time, it would turn into a new life. A baby.

My baby.

But if I kept it, I could be damning us both to a more difficult existence, up to and including possible homelessness. It was one thing for me to suffer, but if my baby suffered and it was my fault? I didn't know if I could ever get over that. It might cause that child to hate me like my own mother hated me. And I didn't know if I could handle that.

All I was left with were impossible decisions.

Finally, I gave up my charade. After forty-eight hours of ducking my roommate by saying I didn't want her to catch my cooties, I went up to Ashley as she made some microwave popcorn.

"Hey, Ash."

"Hey," she smiled over at me like her mom might. Kindly. "You feeling any better?"

"Uh, I have something to confess," I said, tugging on one of my tight curls. "I wasn't actually sick. Well, at least not in that way."

"Okay…"

"I'm ..." God, I pictured the incredulous expression on Trevor's face and almost lost my nerve.

"You're what, Jess?" She put a soothing hand on my arm. "You're starting to scare me now."

I took a deep inhale and blew it out of my mouth. "I'm pregnant."

"Oh, honey," she wrapped her arms around me and hugged me tight. My eyes prickled. Ashley had stayed my friend through thick and thin. I should've known she wouldn't toss me out onto the streets when I gave her distressing news.

She wasn't my mother.

"I want to keep it, but I don't know how to make that work."

"Don't worry. We'll figure it out. How far along are you?"

I winced. "Three months, give or take."

Ashley's jaw dropped. "Have you known all this—"

But I interrupted her, not wanting my best friend to think I'd go so long without telling her something so important. "I just found out. You know how my periods are irregular?"

She nodded.

"Well, I didn't think anything of how I was feeling until you mentioned your aunt being pregnant. And even then, I didn't want to seriously consider it. But I got a couple of stick tests and…"

"And you are."

I nodded.

"I have an appointment tomorrow, and I'm terrified. Will you go with me?"

"Of course, I will." She continued to hold me for a long minute, then asked, "Who's the dad, if you don't mind my asking?"

"Remember that date I had where we went out really nice?"

"Yeah. You guys hooked up, obviously."

"Obviously," I expelled a mirthless chuckle. I hadn't mentioned anything about the Wish Maker's involvement, nor did I intend to. Abruptly, it occurred to me that if my mother ever caught privy to that night, she'd call me a whore again. And this time, she might even be right.

God.

"Are you going to tell him?"

My eyes prickled again. Dammit. "Already tried."

"Didn't go well, I take it."

"No," I choked out. Stupid hitching chest with my stupid wet eyes that wouldn't quit tearing up.

"Well, fuck him."

I jerked my head up so fast I might've caused myself some whiplash. Ashley never cursed. *Ever*. Without being able to stop it, I barked out a blast of laughter.

"Damn, Ash!"

She blushed deeply, the color running all the way from her forehead to her neck.

"I'm just so sick and tired of the people in your life dumping on you."

"You've never once done that," I reminded her, finding a smile.

"And I never will."

My best friend was as good as her word, of course. She went with me to the doctor, then we journeyed to a local thrift store so I could buy a couple of maternity outfits. My future might be chock full of frightening prospects and total unknowns, but I felt better knowing I didn't have to go through it all alone.

10

TREVOR

FEBRUARY

It'd been a month since Jessie Souza had come to my door, and I couldn't keep from mulling the whole conversation—as well as our night together—over in my mind. As usual, I'd been working a gazillion hours a week, so mostly, I was too busy to focus on anything else.

Still, at odd moments she would sneak in there unbidden. When I was awake and firing on all cylinders, I'd remember how pissed I was at her late-night intrusion. I remained uncertain about how she hunted down my private address. Why she'd sought me out only to leave empty-handed.

I'd planned to rip the Wish Maker a new one, but I never followed through. The truth was, I was beginning to contemplate whether or not I'd somehow fucked up and impregnated my date for real.

Because I'd definitely used a condom. I always did. But things had gotten a little out of hand that night. I remembered every detail of it as clear as day, often reliving some of the steamier scenes with my hand finishing me off in my shower.

After dinner, one of the Wish Maker's drivers had taken us to the hotel—I preferred not to use my own Lexus SUV at times like this—and we'd absconded into a room with a durable bed. Back at home, I'd always used Hotel Peter and Paul because all their bed frames were made out of rugged wrought iron. It made placing a woman in restraints easy.

Here in the Big Apple, the Wish Maker had set us up in the Sixty Soho. The hotel was predictably near Soho, but location didn't matter. What mattered was the sturdy four-poster beam construction suspended over the queen-sized mattress. Those beams were four inches thick and solid to the core.

Talk about perfect for my purposes.

And they were. They so were.

We'd gotten past any awkwardness and were communicating well, joking around and making quips back and forth. Jessica was my favorite type of date. She gave as good as she got, and she did it with this endearing half-smile that knocked my socks off.

Fast forward to the main event.

We'd kissed on the couch for a while—I like a good warm-up—then I'd discussed the terms of our evening. I'd suggested the safe word be "flower" simply because there'd been a huge spray of them down in the lobby.

I'd told her not to hesitate to use it, because I did not get off on actual pain. If anything, if what I was doing became too much for her, she was to say the safe word, and everything would immediately halt. It didn't matter that I was paying her for her time. It would stop. I made certain she fully understood that.

I'd enjoyed stripping her bare. Even with that mandarin dress covering everything so modestly, I'd known what was beneath that silky fabric would be extraordinary. And, of course, I'd been right. Luscious tanned skin all over her. Plump lips and breasts with delectably dark nipples that made me go from hard to harder than I'd ever been before.

For a moment there, I'd wondered if I might even pass out. How much blood could a brain lose and still keep a man alive, anyway?

She'd been such a sight to behold laying there on those white sheets, her body laid out on display. And once I brought out the silken rope I kept stockpiled discreetly in my home closet, her breath had come in quick bursts that made her breasts jiggle in the most delicious way. She'd looked nervous, but since all of her was exposed to me, including her glistening pink center, I knew she was just as turned on as she was nervous. Maybe more.

So I'd tied her into place, arms over her head and legs in a wide V. Then, I'd blindfolded her. Next, I stroked myself because … damn. I couldn't help it. I'd been with a lot of women. Likely over a hundred. But there was something about Jessica Isabelle Souza that called out to me like no one else.

I couldn't even say precisely what it was. Her exceptional looks. Her wild curly hair. Her natural yet honeyed scent. But whatever it was, I was aching and leaking for her before we even started, especially when she bit her lip.

I'd had to concentrate and redirect my focus. The dominant must always maintain absolute control at any given time not only to provide the heights of pleasure, but also for safety reasons. What could start out as a light paddling could become a violent thrashing if a dom lost himself—or herself—in the act. Desire has a will of its own. So discipline is essential.

The first thing I'd done is place my erection at her lips. "Do you feel that?"

"Yes," she'd said.

"How does it feel?"

"Hard," she'd answered, just like I'd wanted. "Yet soft. Warm."

"Would you like a taste?"

"Yes, please."

"You may take one, then."

And when her pink tongue flicked out and over the crown of me, I'd had to bite back a groan. I didn't like to be vocal until the end, but whether it was her or the fact that I'd been behaving like a monk for a while, this was proving to be a challenge. So I decided to do something I never had. I decided to relieve some pressure right there at the beginning.

Leaning over her with one knee of the bed, I pushed closer to her. "Kiss it," I told her next. Then, "Suck it. Take the whole head."

She had a small mouth and I'm both long and thick, so I knew any deep throat action would be out of the question. But that didn't mean she couldn't give me what I wanted. She was sucking on me carefully, too carefully for my tastes, but I still rewarded her for obeying without hesitation by kneading both her breasts. She moaned around me, and I closed my eyes, doing my best to maintain.

Yeah, I was going to have to relieve that pressure for sure.

I reached down into her core, fingering her up and down until her moans became a constant unending hum. Then, I circled her clit over and over with light pressure, then with greater and greater amounts of resistance until I could feel her starting to throb against my fingertips.

"I know you need to come, but you have to wait until I say," I teased her, coaxing her orgasm out towards release at the same time. "Wait for it. Wait. Wait." Then I thrust two fingers inside of her all at once, pressing the flat of my palm to her folds as my thumb rubbed her clit. "Come for me, Jessica. Come for me. *Now.*"

She did and it was beautiful. Restrained as she was, she couldn't fling her body around as much as she clearly would have otherwise but feeling her pulse on my hand had me right at my limits. I held off as long as I could, the bulbous head of me still in her mouth, then I told her to suck on me harder.

"That's it. Take as much of me as you can. Then, you're going to swallow me down. Do you understand?"

She nodded, and that was all it took. "Now," I growled out in warning, shooting down her throat, groaning as she swallowed around me once, twice, and then again.

"Lick me clean," I ordered her, though my voice was shaky after that. Regardless, I was still hard and still wanted more of her, even after coming like I had. I blinked, taking several deep breaths. Damn, that was good.

Then, I pulled away. This was one of my favorite parts, the phase I called torture. It involved me dragging my fingers along every inch of her skin, drawing circular patterns as I went. I always loved it when they squirmed, usually because they were ticklish, and when Jessica jerked backwards when I taunted the side of her rib cage, I knew I had her.

"Huh-uh. That's a bad, bad Jessica. You were supposed to hold totally still, remember?"

"It tickles," she said, biting her lip and skittering away from my hand, which just meant I would continue to do it.

"Now you're being bad again. What are the rules?"

The rules were that unless I told her to say something else, her answers were always to be either yes sir or no sir. She repeated this to me, and I shifted the ropes on the beams at the bottom of the bed until her ass was partially exposed.

"Bad girls get spanked, so I'm going to spank you now. Three smacks. Here we go." I had a strategy for this. I aimed my hand at such an angle that it would hit both her ass and the bottom portion of her core. The intention was for it to be eighty to ninety percent pleasure to twenty to ten percent pain. It was all about how hard I hit her.

"Count them for me." I smacked her once, enough for her to feel it and for it to make noise, but not enough for her to flinch.

"One."

I smacked her a second time, this time with a resounding slapping noise. That one should've stung a bit, and from her gasp, I could tell it had.

"Two," she said, breathlessly.

This last one could be tricky. It would be softer than the other two but because she was already tender, it could still hurt if not measured out precisely. I could sense that she had more delicate, sensitive skin, so I when I smacked her, I barely touched her. Even still, she gasped anyway.

"Three," she whispered, her chest hitching.

Correction: very sensitive skin. I'd have to be even more cautious than I customarily was.

No problem.

She's worth it. The thought bounced around my brain. I agreed. I was also proud of her; she hadn't flinched away at all.

"Good girl," I murmured into her ear, before kneeling halfway off the bed. Ever since I'd seen her smoothly shaven core, I'd felt a desire to taste her, so taste her I did, with one languorous lick of my tongue.

And *yum*. She was earthy, and even better, tasted as amazing as she smelled. That honeyed essence wasn't just in my nose, it was on my taste buds, and I lapped her up, glorying in the sensuality of it all. With her legs still raised partially in the air, I had a great vantage point and so I positioned myself almost lazily on my side. I licked at her folds as my two fingers slid inside her. It was a motion I'd be repeating with another body part soon.

She went higher and higher, her core becoming wetter and wetter, and it was so delicious. With her thighs surrounding my head, her soft skin *everywhere*, I couldn't imagine any other place I could ever want to be. Despite relieving the pressure, I wanted her again, but this time I needed to be inside her when I came.

Stepping away for long enough to shield myself with a condom, I returned and slid inch by inch inside of her. Despite her being so ready for me, I gave her time to adjust. She was so hot and so tight I had to hold my breath to keep from going too far too fast. I even forgot myself for a second and fell out of character, my hands on her hips.

"Relax for me, baby. Just relax."

Shit. I hadn't meant to do that. Speak soft words to her like a lover. So I brought back the same harshness to my voice as I'd been using all along. I'd managed to sink into her completely by now, anyway. No harm done.

"Open your legs wider," I commanded her, and she stretched out for me, making me groan again. Had I ever been inside a woman this tight before?

I didn't think so.

Then, I started to move, and within moments, she began to flutter around me.

"Here, suck on these," I told her, offering her the two fingers I'd had inside her a moment ago. I wanted to see her face when she tasted herself.

She appeared hesitant at first, as if this was weird for her. But then, she suckled them with gusto as she moved beneath me. I wanted to feel her come around me, and I wanted it to be so entrancing that she let go completely. I thrusted into her, being vigilant about staying within her tolerance threshold. I could feel her flutters becoming vibrations, so I took advantage of it, moving faster.

"I want you to come again. Come, Jessica. Now!" And again, she did, calling out in a noisy keen that shook the picture frames on the walls.

I fucking loved it.

Maybe too much, because I wanted it to continue. I wanted her to come over and over until she forgot her name. Until she only knew one name.

Mine.

So I increased my pace and the pressure I used to enter her. Yanking myself nearly out of her, I pushed right back in, this time all at once. But it wasn't enough. She'd scrunched up her features, but I didn't stop. I wanted more, more, more. She hit another peak and then another. And I kept going. At last, on her fourth—or was it her fifth?—she cried out in a raspy voice.

"Trevor, oh God, *Trevor!*"

I pounded into her, not holding back in the least as I rutted out my climax over her like an animal. I saw spots before my eyes and was breathing like an asthmatic as I fell onto the bed, pushing myself over far enough not to crush her.

Never in my life had I come so hard.

I was whisked back to my present reality because of discomfort. The memory of that night had caused my shaft to grow thick and heavy enough between my legs that it rubbed up against the confines of my zipper. But then, this happened anytime I allowed myself to relive it from start to earth-shattering finish.

But had there been any issue with that condom?

I tried to think back, to visualize myself inspecting it. But the truth was, I hadn't. Like so many times before, I'd taken a tissue and thrown it away. I didn't think it'd been torn or damaged in any way, but could I be sure?

Nope.

No matter how much I wanted to discount the visit I'd received from Jessie Souza, I kept circling back around to a few crucial points. She told me she was pregnant, that she hadn't been with anyone else, and then, she hadn't asked me for a thing. Not one thing. Yet, I hadn't believed her.

Should I?

If there was even the slightest possibility that she was legitimately carrying my child, shouldn't I know it? Shouldn't I do what was necessary? Shouldn't I man up and offer her some help, even if the idea of it freaked me the fuck out?

Deep down, I felt like I already knew the answer, but to stall, I decided to get another opinion.

"Trevor," Jax answered on the third ring. "Long time, no call."

"I know," I apologized. "Things have been off the chain here."

"Try having a couple of kids." He chuckled out, and since that made a convenient segue, I pounced on it.

"Uh, speaking of kids. How did you know when Roxy was pregnant?"

That time, he laughed out loud. "Dude, really?"

"Yes, really," I shot back him, feeling surly. If it was true, it wasn't funny. Not at all. Especially given how I left things with her.

"Well, she told me, of course," Jax said, residual humor in his tone. "And then, you know, everything changes."

"What do you mean, everything?"

"Like, obviously, her belly expands to make room for the baby. But the way she interacted with me changed, too. The way she felt both physically and emotionally changed. She was a little bit nauseous in the beginning. And certain parts of her were sore sometimes. She'd cry at the most minor thing, like a commercial or even a cute onesie that said, 'Daddy's Second in Command.'"

"Okay," I said. "But like …" I didn't know what I was really asking, or maybe, how to phrase what I needed to know. "If you'd had a woman approach you way after a hookup to tell you that she was about to have your kid, how would you respond to that?"

There was a pause. "How pregnant did she say she was? Do the times match up?"

"Well," I contemplated this. "That's one of my issues. If she's being honest with me, she should be like, four months along now."

"Does she look pregnant?"

"Uh …" How did I tell him I hadn't seen her in a month without sounding like a dick? "She didn't."

"When did you see her last?"

I rubbed the back of my neck, which suddenly felt kind of hot. "Mid-January."

"All right, it's a couple weeks into February now, so …" he muttered under his breath. "Hey, Rox, come here a sec, would you?"

I heard some muffled voices, then, "Well, with Alec, she started to show at three months. Just an adorable little pooch." Evidently, his wife remained within earshot. "With Callie, though, she said she didn't look pregnant until she was about four months in. There's a bunch of stuff about first pregnancies as opposed to additional pregnancies and girls being carried differently than boys that I won't go into. But my guess would be that most women start to show at around three to four months."

"Cool," I said automatically, feeling numb.

"And FYI? Condoms aren't one hundred percent safe. Just sayin'."

"Oh." That was news to me. Bad news. "Uh, thanks for all the info."

"Good luck, man. Let me know how everything turns out."

The conversation with my best friend served an important purpose. It made me realize I needed to visit Jessie Souza again. I needed to know definitively if she was pregnant or not.

I honestly didn't know at this point which outcome I wanted. If her stomach still seemed flat as a fritter, that would mean she'd been lying to me. Yet if the opposite was true, that would mean that not only was I assured of permanent douche-hood, but also that I was most likely the father.

Either way, I'd feel like shit.

Christ.

11

JESSIE

We were in the cool down section of my Zumba class, and I was grateful. Though I'd been lucky enough to experience almost no morning sickness, this overwhelming fatigue crap would just not go away. I felt lethargic at best, and downright exhausted the rest of the time. I'd started to sleep for more lengthy stints of time at night, and when I could, I also tried to get at least a thirty-minute nap in the early afternoon. But there wasn't always time for such things.

I'd made the decision to pull out of my student teaching and my other courses this semester. With the baby coming, I had to save as much money as I could ahead of time. It depressed me to be so close to obtaining my degree only to have to put it off, but I knew a deferment was a reasonable compromise.

Thank God for Ashley.

She'd been nothing but patient and supportive. She'd even insisted on switching rooms with me. Hers was bigger than mine by about five square feet, and that extra space would be just enough to fit a crib in the corner. Ashley was way too good to me. I didn't deserve her.

But I'd feel forever grateful for her.

And great, now I was crying in the midst of a Zumba session. Well, not in the midst, but the class hadn't finished yet. What a mess. I wiped the sweat from my forehead while surreptitiously swiping at my eyes. If I was lucky, none of my students would think anything of it.

Right after brushing away my tears, I glanced up to see an apparition in the mirror. I squinted my eyes closed and opened them again, expecting it to be gone, but it was still there. I turned my head, and sure enough the apparition remained. Only it wasn't an apparition at all.

It was Trevor.

The first thought that went through my head was, *What the ever-loving fuck?* The second was Ashley's contribution: *Cheese and crackers!* Neither seemed sufficient enough to describe the tumult of thoughts and emotions rattling around inside my skull, though.

Not even close.

I fell out of step with everyone else and had a hard time getting back into a normal rhythm. The music continued to blare out from the speakers overhead, so I tried again. And again. But it was a lost cause. I stepped out of formation and dropped to one knee, retying my perfectly tied shoelaces. I took my time, and eventually, the music tapered to a stop. Everyone broke off, going their separate ways.

Only once everyone had departed did Trevor approach me.

I spent that time digging through my duffle bag. I didn't know why he was here, but I didn't want to feel humiliated again. With my hormones being all over the place, I cried at the drop of a hat—just like I had moments before—and I didn't want to cry in front of him. It was horrible enough that he didn't believe this baby was his. I didn't need to give him any additional psychological weaponry to use against me.

"Jessica, I mean, Jessie. Hi," he said, and I peered up at him, noticing that he appeared antsy and unsure. That was new. He also wasn't meeting my eye.

I stood to my full five-foot one-inch height. It didn't help me feel any more powerful really. But it did capture Trevor's attention. In fact, every single bit of his attention went to one portion of my anatomy. My baby bump.

I'd peeled off the oversized t-shirt I wore over my spandex workout clothes these days, the one I used to camouflage my condition. Once it was gone my pregnancy became more than evident, even though I wasn't anywhere near as round as I knew I'd grow to be.

Soon, I wouldn't be able to hide anything anymore, and I'd have to explain that I was expecting to my students. It might not end up being that big a deal, but I wasn't ready to reveal this yet.

Once they knew, some of the nosier women would likely pepper me with queries I might not feel comfortable answering. Including ones about whether or not I could continue to be their instructor long term. I didn't know the answer to that, so I was putting that conversation off for as long as possible.

"How did you find me?" I asked him.

"Wasn't that difficult. I Googled your name and saw you listed as a fitness instructor."

"Oh."

There was a long and deafening silence.

"How did you find me last month, if you don't mind me asking?" he asked, finally.

"You uh ... left a receipt behind. Back at the hotel. Must've fallen out of your pocket. It was for a pizza and wings."

His lips lifted into a faint semblance of a grin. "My favorite meal."

"You like pineapple on your pizza," I observed.

"Yeah. You ever tried it?"

"No."

"You should. You might like it," he said, rubbing the back of his neck.

Why the hell were we discussing pineapple at a time like this?

"Why are you here?" I asked, needing him to get to the point.

"I wanted to see you. Needed to." His eyes lowered to my tummy again.

Ah. I felt a sharp rush of indignation and couldn't help gritting my teeth. "This isn't padding, if that's what think."

"I believe you," he admitted quietly, but I didn't know what he meant by that.

"You believe me about what?" my voice double the volume of his.

"About you being pregnant. And about it being mine."

"When did you come to this brilliant conclusion?" I was being snippy, I knew. But I couldn't seem to help myself.

"I …" He hesitated, and I was again struck by his apparent loss of confidence. I didn't know if I liked this humbler version of him or not. "I've been thinking about it continually over the past month. I'm sorry I was so … nasty to you when you came by. I have no excuse for my behavior."

Maybe his contriteness shouldn't have softened me toward him, but it did. "It must've been a shock to your system. I know it was to mine. If you want it, I can request a paternity test from my doctor."

"That's okay. I know the timing lines up." No denying that, at least. Good to know he was willing to admit it. "So, are you and … and the baby okay?"

"We're good so far."

"Do you have like, any doctor's appointments coming up?"

He wanted to know about my appointments?

"Yeah."

"Can I join you on the next one? I know it's a lot to ask, but if it's okay, I'd like to be involved."

My mouth dropped open. After our previous little soirée, I'd pretty much ascertained that he wanted no part of this. I mean, what kind of man would ever acknowledge a son or daughter conceived the way ours was? I didn't like to ruminate on the fact that I'd gotten pregnant while getting paid to have sex, but it was exactly what had happened. I'd done it for the money, expecting it to be terrible. But then, it hadn't been.

The truth was, up until I'd discovered this pregnancy, when I thought about that night with Trevor, certain aspects of it made me smile. Even though for the sake of my sanity I'd decided to never do it again, I'd liked being with him. We'd both gone into the arrangement with our eyes wide open. It's just that we hadn't anticipated any far-reaching consequences.

Especially not something like this.

"I suppose that would be okay," I replied. I'd told him because I'd wanted him to know. This baby was his, and I couldn't in good conscience push him away now.

"Awesome." He smiled at me, then, and it was the same charming smile he'd given me on our date together. This one, though, rather than melting my knees and making my nipples stand on end, was friendlier and more affable. Sweeter.

Which was an ironic way to think about a man who'd secured me to a bed with actual ropes, ordered me to obey him, and had proceeded to fuck me until I screamed his name.

I'd had so many orgasms in that hotel room that I'd nearly blacked out. Maybe it shouldn't have come as such a surprise that he'd impregnated me. I didn't know much about Trevor, but I knew he was potent.

In more ways than one.

"It's this Thursday," I said. "At three in the afternoon."

"I'll be there," he promised.

And now, I'd just have to see if he actually would.

12

TREVOR

As I took in the reflective black glass doors, my pulse did this peculiar act of galloping like a horse before stuttering out completely, only to do it again. And again. It was like the unsynchronized rhythm of some nerdy guy who couldn't dance to save his life. Were pulse rates supposed to do such things? Race and then stop? Because that was what mine was doing, and it was making me feel lightheaded.

Or maybe it's what I was facing inside that made me feel that way.

The sign above me said one word. *Womancare*. It sounded like a spa or something to me, but actually, this would be where women went for gynecological and obstetrical checkups. This place was all about a woman's reproductive health and the health of any children she may be having. I knew this not because I was experienced or wise, but because I'd Googled it.

I'd always considered myself to be a pretty worldly person on top of being intelligent. I'd taken trips to Europe and Asia. I had my MBA. Though I loved my football, I'd also been exposed to the Met and had seen a couple of shows on Broadway. I wasn't some uncultured Neanderthal.

Yet, I'd had no idea when I'd gotten out of my taxi and looked up to see the Womancare sign if I was in the right location or not. And then, I realized I didn't even know what I was about to see, so I'd done some last-minute online research. I'd had so much sex with women but knew squat about what they had to do to take care of themselves.

It didn't make me feel as evolved as I thought I'd been.

I'd read about all these different forms of birth control. The only two methods I was really familiar with at all were the pill and condoms. Oops. And then I started to read about all the stuff involved once a woman conceives a child. All the mood swings and tiredness. The sore swollen nipples and stretch marks and back pain. My ignorance threw me for one hell of a loop.

I was actually quaking in my boots when I thought about the process of labor and delivery. I hadn't read much about that yet. I'd seriously considered getting hammered before I came here, which made me comprehend just how much of a jackass I'd been up to this point.

And so far, Jessica had gone through all this by herself.

It made me feel like an insensitive prick of an asshole, and even that insult didn't seem to cover it. Although I'd already apologized to her at her gym, I knew I needed to do it again. In fact, I didn't know how many more apologizes I owed her. Several more, at least. I'd fucked up that badly.

Talk about eating some humble pie.

Her appointment wasn't scheduled for another twenty-five minutes, but I entered the automatic doors anyway, needing to do something with myself. There was a booth at the front manned by a large lady with hair so unnaturally bright pink it must be a dye job, and she glanced up at me suspiciously as the doors swished closed behind me.

"Can I help you, sir?"

"Yes. My uh …" I trailed off, feeling stumped. I was sure this receptionist thought I was either in the wrong place, was some creepoid, or was a husband or boyfriend of one of the patients here. What did I say now, since I was none of the above? If I gave her an incorrect answer, would she call security on me? Christ, I'd never felt more insecure in my life.

"Jessie Souza has a three o'clock appointment here?" I presented this as a question. Nice.

Not.

"And Jessie Souza is?" she prompted, her long manicured fingernails—the same color as her flamboyant hair—poised to type something on her keyboard.

What sort of response was she looking for? "Pregnant?"

She blinked what had to be false eyelashes at me. "Okay, but that's not what I was asking. I need some more information from you. What's her doctor's name?"

Well, *fuck*. "I don't know."

"And you are?"

"Trevor Keller."

"No, I mean what is your relation to the patient?"

"Uh …" Somehow, I didn't think saying that she was my one-time hookup would win me any brownie points. "I'm her baby's father."

It was strange to say those words. This was my first time admitting it out loud, and I waited to see if it would feel like a lie. It didn't. Somewhere between the time I saw Jessica's slightly rounded abdomen and now, five days later, I'd come to accept her story. She could still be pulling the wool over my eyes, but deep down, I didn't think so. My instincts were insisting that she'd told me the truth.

"All right, then." She tapped something into the computer, her fingernails flying. How the hell did she type with those talons sticking out like that? "Go up to the third floor and turn left. You're looking for suite 304."

"Thanks."

Feeling too on edge to take a sedate and slow elevator ride up such a short distance, I headed for the stairs, taking them two at a time. The walls were painted a grayish blue, a shade probably meant to be calming, though I couldn't say it made much difference to me personally. On the way, I caught sight of artwork that helped identify exactly what this place was.

There were paintings of women holding small children, stills of bare pregnant bellies, and posters showing inkblots of miniature hands and feet. There were women in yoga poses, silhouettes of families holding hands—dad on one side, mom on the other, with a couple of little ones in between—as well as a charcoal drawing of a mother breastfeeding.

Was it truly okay for me to be here?

Things only became worse once I found suite 304. Here, there were pamphlets about in vitro fertilization, intrauterine devices, and something called a vaginal ring. There was even a fucking diagram of a magnified uterus on one of the walls, right between a Ficus tree and a water fountain. As if displaying giant-sized wombs was the most normal thing in the world.

What was I doing here again?

Jessica. Supporting Jessica. That's what I was doing. But what if she didn't show up? What if this was some sick prank?

Jesus, I was losing it.

As I paced back and forth, a woman waddled in appearing as if she'd swallowed a pumpkin. A colossal one. She was followed by another woman, her baby bump not pumpkin-sized, but definitely larger than Jessica's.

I kept glancing up and catching sight of that damn uterus. Finally, I made myself sit down with my back to it. I took a couple of cleansing breaths and told myself to settle down. Having a panic attack in front of a bunch of knocked up strangers had not been on the agenda for today. I peered at my watch, wondering if she was late, but only fifteen minutes had passed.

How had all this drama happened inside my head in fifteen measly minutes?

Seriously, Keller. Get. A. Grip.

Just a couple moments after that, a set of familiar black curls appeared. Thank God.

Jessica stared at me for one endless moment, her mouth gaping as if astonished. Then, she went to the desk at the far side of the room to confirm her appointment. When she turned back around, I had this sinking feeling that she wasn't going to sit with me.

I mean, I had basically treated her like pond scum when she'd come to inform me of my impending fatherhood, so maybe I deserved her snub. Who was I kidding? I *absolutely* deserved it. But why would she invite me to her appointment only to give me the silent treatment? For what felt like the twenty-fifth time today, I was anxious.

I didn't like the feeling.

Just when I thought she'd shut me out, she veered toward the water fountain, and two and two became four. I jumped up to beat her to it, grabbing one of those paper cups and filling it for her. I offered her the cup, hoping to prove that I could be gallant when the occasion called for it. But I knew it'd take more than a single time of anticipating her needs before she'd forgive me. *If* she could forgive me.

We'd just sat down—together—when a voice said, "Ms. Souza?" We hopped to our feet again.

The nurse—I'm assuming she was a nurse based on the fact that she wore pink scrubs with storks on them—led us through a labyrinthine hallway to a tiny private room. "Since we're doing your first sonogram today, there's no need to strip down this time. Dr. Carrey will be with you shortly." Then, the nurse shut the door behind us, leaving us alone in the room together.

Jessica seemed just as uncomfortable as I felt. Needing something to do, I offered to take her coat. She gave it to me mutely, then went to sit on the exam table. I noticed that unlike other physician's tables, this one had metal doohickeys sticking out of the bottom.

Stirrups, my brain provided, accessing the pages of research I'd recently gulped down. For the woman to rest her feet in. I'd only ever seen stirrups on silly sitcoms. Then, they'd been an excuse for the audience to laugh—cue Ross from *Friends* getting trapped in them—but being within inches of the genuine articles now didn't feel at all like a laughing matter.

Shit was getting real.

I was still standing there, her coat over my arm, and feeling like an idiot, when a light knock issued from the door. "Hi, there, Jessie."

"Hi," she said, her voice small. "Uh, this is Trevor. He's the father."

I wondered if her physician would ask me where I'd been up till now or even make a scathing remark, but she didn't.

"Are you two ready to see your baby for the first time?"

"Yes," Jessica said, sounding surer of herself than she had before. My mouth went dry at the query, so I only nodded.

"How have you been feeling, Jessie?" the doctor asked her, and I felt like a chump for not inquiring myself.

"Okay."

"Any pain?"

"No, not really."

"Any nausea or fatigue?"

"Fatigue," Jessica stated, rubbing her eyes. "I don't seem to have any energy at all. I'm sleeping more, but it isn't helping."

Worry threaded itself around my spine and flooded my system like venom from a poisonous snake. Did that mean something was wrong? But before I could ask, Dr. Carrey patted her patient's arm and answered.

"Fatigue is a common symptom of pregnancy. Sometimes it lets up during the second trimester and returns in the third, and sometimes, it stays with you throughout. The main thing I would encourage is a healthy diet with lots of vegetables and fruits. Also, have you been taking your prenatal vitamins?"

"I ran out," Jessica admitted.

"I'll get you some," I put in, and she gawked at me as if I'd just told her I'd come up with the cure to cancer. "Is it a prescription?"

"No," Dr. Carrey responded this time. "They're available at any pharmacy and most grocery stores."

I took out my phone and opened my notes app, jotting this down.

The nurse came back in with some sort of scanning apparatus, and I watched as they raised Jessica's shirt, exposing her stomach. Seeing her bare and bulging belly further cemented that she was unequivocally with child, and I observed the proceedings, entranced by what they were doing.

Once everything was set up, the doctor took a tube of KY jelly and squirted it on Jessica's skin. Then, using a plastic wand, she ran the device across the lowest part of her abdomen. A staticky sound immediately filled the room. The noises had a regular yet sloshy cadence, and I had to speak up again.

"What are we hearing?"

"That's the baby's heartbeat."

Holy crap!

"Is that sound normal?" I asked, my own heart rapping hard against my rib cage. "Is it healthy?"

Dr. Carrey smiled at my enthusiasm. "Yes, this is a normal fetal heartbeat. And yes, all indications so far are that this baby is healthy."

"How far along is she exactly?" I asked next, ready to type it into my notes.

"Based on the size of the head, she's now at seventeen weeks."

"I still haven't felt anything," Jessica spoke up. "My pregnancy books say I should start to feel life anytime now."

"It varies from woman to woman. It usually feels like a soft fluttering this early, some mothers compare it to butterfly wings. Keep paying attention, and you'll feel it," Dr. Carrey assured her.

"So that means the baby is due when?" I asked, reentering the conversation.

The nurse pulled up a screen on the desktop computer. "Official predicted due date is July 25th."

"A summer baby," the physician added, but all I could think about was how July wasn't that far away. "And there he or she is."

She pointed at a black, white, and gray image on the monitor attached to the scanning machine, moving the wand back and forth. I squinted at it, and then, miraculously, I detected the clear outline of a miniature hand shaped like a starfish, and Jesus Christ, a *face*. There was a nose and ears and a mouth. The corners of my eyes stung, and the back of my throat became hot. I was staring at Jessica's baby, at *my* baby.

I cleared my throat, taking an audibly shaky breath. In my peripheral vision, I noticed Jessica wiping her eyes, and I avoided meeting her gaze. Damn, I couldn't lose it if she was. She needed me to be strong, and here I was barely keeping myself in check. In an attempt to keep all my unruly emotions at bay, I zeroed in on getting more information.

"What's the gender?" My voice sounded like a bullfrog's but if anyone noticed, they were kind enough not to remark on it.

"Let's see if we can tell ..." Dr. Carrey swept the wand over a certain area of Jessica's stomach, and the screen filled with the distinct picture of two round globes, like a pressed ham. "Listen, little one, we'd all like to know what you are, so we'd appreciate it if you'd cooperate."

But no matter what the doctor did, the baby wouldn't position itself in the correct way for anything between its legs to be identifiable. Rather than being upset or disappointed, however, I chuckled.

"Is it ... *mooning* us right now?" I asked.

The doctor stilled and grinned back at me. "That's precisely what he or she is doing. Tell me, does stubbornness run in either of your families?"

At that, I laughed out loud. "It does. It's part and parcel of the Keller DNA. And the mooning thing ... That baby *must* belong to me."

Up to that point, I'd been concentrating on the amazing creature squirming on the monitor, but now I looked directly at Jessica. She was staring at me with weepy jade green eyes, so many emotions swimming there I couldn't possibly read them all.

I felt an impulse to clasp her hand in mine, and I did, hoping she wouldn't reject my touch. She didn't. Instead, she tightened her grip. Something important happened between us in that moment. Something beyond anything that had transpired until then. I felt linked to her, connected to her in a way I'd never been to anyone else.

Wow.

Dr. Carrey began talking again, but I missed the beginning of what she said. What I caught was, "... and since you experienced a miscarriage once before, this pregnancy is considered high risk..."

"Wait... you had a miscarriage?" I asked Jessica, interrupting her doctor who instantly went silent as the grave. I got the feeling that her physician had just told me something she wasn't supposed to, but I didn't care. I needed to know, confidentiality be damned.

Jessica sighed, her features wreathed in sorrow.

Abruptly, her doctor spoke again, her voice extra cheery. "Well, Nurse Tyra and I will go get you some printouts from your sonogram. We'll be back in a jiffy." They each scurried out, but I only had eyes for their patient.

"I did," Jessica shuddered out, breaking eye contact. "When I was seventeen. I wasn't in a situation where I could get the proper medical care. I started bleeding and by the time I arrived at the emergency room, there was nothing they could do to stop it."

She sounded sad, but there was more there, too. I almost pushed for more but decided against it. I didn't have the right to ask about her past. What I had to do was protect the part of her life that was currently intersecting with mine.

"That won't happen this time," I told her in a bolstering voice, though I needed to bolster myself as much as I did her. "I won't let it. Anything you need, day or night, you call me. I'm sorry you went through that before, and I'm sorry that you're in this position now because of me. But I want you to be safe, and I want our baby to be safe. So even though my track record isn't the best, I'm going to take care of you both, okay?"

"I appreciate that," she said. "But I'm not looking for some sort of payout from you."

The subject of money was a tricky one for us, for obvious reasons. But I had the means to provide the best of care and that's what I was going to do. "This is my responsibility, Jessica. One I would never shirk. I expect you to let me to at least pay for all the medical costs. It's what any decent father would do, and it's only fair."

She chewed on her bottom lip, reminding me of our night together. As casually as I could, I shifted my position, annoyed at my body rising to the occasion at such an inappropriate time. We'd already been there, done that together. That's what put us into this precarious position to begin with, and it was time that my overzealous libido got the memo.

"All right," she relented.

"Thank you for letting me be with you today."

"I'm glad you're here."

Teardrops coated her eyelashes and the connection to her I felt earlier increased in strength. It must be because of the baby. We may have started on this journey together inadvertently, but now that we'd created this precious new lifeform together we needed to develop better communication skills.

We'd have to have lots of discussions back and forth over the coming months. Once the baby was born, we'd need to be open enough to interact about custody and other vital issues. Even if it was too early to discuss all that just yet.

Usually, I thought time passed slowly, but July was just around the corner. We had to prepare, and it would probably benefit each of us to know one another better, and not in the biblical sense.

"How about we agree to a couple of weekly lunches on me, say Mondays and Fridays at one? You pick the place. I'll go to all your appointments and be open to anything else you want my input on. Would that work for you?"

She visibly relaxed. "I'd like that."

"Got your phone?" She handed it over and I programmed it with my number, then sent a text from hers. Now we were officially in each other's contact lists. "Just let me know where you want to meet and whether you'd like me to pick you up."

Dr. Carrey arrived with the sonogram pics, and we both stared at them for a minute, stunned by the enormity of what we saw. My heart pounded in my chest, not with fear, but with love for my child. I hadn't known I could feel this way about anything or anyone, and again, I had to force myself to blink back the burning behind my eyes.

Maybe our circumstances weren't ideal, but for that palm-sized human being, we needed to learn how to get along. We'd have to make this work somehow.

One way or another.

13

JESSIE

On the day of my sonogram appointment, I discovered something I never would've considered prior to then: It would be dangerously easy to fall for a man like Trevor Keller.

Not that I ever would.

And there was even less of a chance that he might fall for me. That kind of stuff only happened in movies and books, not in reality. But when he'd promised that he would do whatever it took to be there for our baby, I just... melted.

He'd probably disappoint me and break that promise somewhere along the way, but I *wanted* to believe that he would do the right thing. More than anything, I'd love it if my baby had the opportunity to grow up with a father, a dedicated man he or she could count on. I wanted a better life for my baby than the one I'd had.

I'd never known who my real biological father was or if he was even aware of my existence. I had no other male family members who were still living. And my mother's boyfriend...

Well, I wasn't about to go there.

So for this baby to have a positive male role model would be a dream come true. The only example I had of such a person was Ashley's dad, even though he'd died when she was six. She had fond memories of him, though. Happy family portraits she'd shown me. She'd loved him and he'd loved her and her mom. I was glad she'd experienced that if only for a short while.

Since my best friend had to attend a meeting, I hopped in the shower and made some frozen chicken nuggets and boxed macaroni and cheese for us. I also pulled a boiled egg out of the fridge, one Ashley had set aside for me. She'd been making several up in batches since I craved eggs all the time now.

It was so sweet of her, especially considering she hated them. When I'd mentioned that she didn't have to go to all that trouble, she'd simply mentioned that the protein was good for me and the baby. I didn't know what I'd do without her.

Ashley had spoiled me so much lately, and I wanted to return the favor, even if this dinner I was preparing for her was nowhere near made from scratch.

"Jess, honey? Where are you?" she called out as soon as she walked in.

I came out of our narrow galley kitchen brandishing the printouts of my sonogram. "Wanna see?"

She beamed at me. "Oooh, gimme gimme!"

Ashley poured over the photos, tracing my baby's profile with an index finger. "So adorable. Could they tell if it was a boy or a girl?"

I gave her the last picture, one I'd been hiding behind my back, and she giggled like a twelve-year-old. I did too, thinking of Trevor's reaction to our baby seemingly mooning us like a drunken frat boy.

"Well," my roomie said, "I take that as a no."

"No. Not this time. But they've scheduled me for another sonogram closer to my delivery date. Maybe the little pill will behave once it's grown some."

"Did the father show?" she asked me next, and I could hear the hesitancy in her tone.

"He did."

"And?"

"And he was great. Really," I told her. Recounting how Trevor had plied Dr. Carrey with twenty questions before promising to be there for the baby. Of course, at that part I got awfully misty-eyed.

"I'm so glad. I worried about you all day."

Ashley had accompanied me on each of my other appointments. She'd been my rock. But today, she'd had a meeting with her academic advisor that she couldn't reschedule. Trevor volunteering to be with me instead had come at the most serendipitous moment.

"Do you think he'll man up and stay by your side?" was her next query, as her gaze assessed me.

"That would be so nice. He said he would and he sounded genuine, but who knows? I guess the proof will be in the pudding."

It would be fantastic if Trevor wound up being as dependable as I needed him to be, but I wasn't about to hold my breath. Still, I allowed my thoughts to wander to the zing of desire I'd felt when he'd held my hand earlier. It was so ridiculous. Getting turned on by a guy innocently pressing his palm to mine—especially when I remembered what else we'd done together—but I had.

I'd felt a powerful pull toward him, one I couldn't deny. But it was probably just a side effect of the pregnancy, right? Hormones gone astray? That must be what it was. My body had begun to feel different, and that frightened me so much. My first pregnancy hadn't progressed to this point, so this was all uncharted territory for me.

Up till today, my concentration had been on problem solving and trying not to panic. Ashley was going to help me, and somehow, I'd go step by step and muddle through. At least, that was what I'd imagined myself doing. Yet when I saw those sonogram images, something warm inside me flowed from my heart and outwards.

When I'd made the decision to keep my baby, it'd been partially because I thought I'd never forgive myself if I got rid of it and partially because ending the pregnancy just felt wrong.

And now, seeing those miniscule fingers and toes…

Seeing the shape of its delicate little head…

It was overwhelming.

For the first time, I realized that I was feeling love for my baby, the deepest kind of love. And somehow, no matter what happened between Trevor and me, I knew I'd do whatever it took to become the best mommy I could.

The first lunch I shared with Trevor was at a local home cooking place that served breakfast all day long. That had been intentional on my part. And when he heard my order, he waited until our server departed, then commented on it.

"An omelet for lunch, huh? With feta cheese, salami, and pickles. Do you always eat in such an unconventional manner or is this the pregnancy talking?" he asked me, quirking his lips upwards.

I answered his question with another question. "You ever watch *Scrubs?*"

"Yeah."

"There's this episode where Turk begs and begs his wife to make him *brinner*, where breakfast is dinner."

His grin widened. "I remember. Are you saying that's you?"

"Yes, but being pregnant has only exacerbated my weird appetite. I think it's the whole egg thing. I can't seem to get enough of them."

"So instead of getting you some takeout pizza, you'd rather I show up with egg fu young or scrambled eggs?"

I tried to visualize this and had to laugh. "Sounds challenging and possibly messy."

"Probably would be. But I'd figure out a way to do it for you."

I peered over at him, feeling like a lovesick puppy. Then, I snapped myself out of it. While I was glad he was being nice to me, this was temporary. He was doing it because I was having his child, not because I personally meant anything to him. I needed to make sure I kept my perspective where he was involved. Time to get back down to what these lunches were supposed to be about.

"So, we're here to get to know one another better, right?"

"Yes," he agreed.

"Let me summarize what I know about you so far. You live in an upscale apartment on the upper east side. You wear suits a lot. You like pizza with pineapple. And you like to ask tons of questions when in an unfamiliar situation. Care to add to that?"

I made a point of leaving certain things unsaid, like the fact that he used the Wish Maker to arrange dates for him, that he liked to pay for sex, and that he was exceedingly demanding and a bit kinky in the bedroom—as well as surprisingly gentle.

Whew, was it suddenly too hot in here? It was forty-five degrees outside, but they must have the heat cranked up in this restaurant. It might even be malfunctioning, since I was sweating. I took the little display they used to advertise current specials and fanned myself with it. Was it just my imagination or had his grin turned wolfish?

"Well," he began, scooting forward in his chair. "I'm an investment banker. I moved here from New Orleans a few months back. I work about a million hours a week to advance my career. Being a success is really important to me."

"Is that why you moved here? Your career?"

"Yes. I worked for a corporation owned by friends of my family for several years, but…" He paused in order to take a long drink of his sweet tea. "That position wasn't taking me where I wanted to go."

"What do investment bankers do?" I asked, not having a clue.

"Besides making money, you mean?" His tone was jovial, but I could tell something more serious underlaid that. "I guess it's about security. When you help others invest wisely, it grows both their capital and their retirement. They grow their portfolios, and I benefit on the fiscal end of things. Knowing you have a nest egg set aside just in case is comforting. I help people have the most profitable nest eggs possible."

I wondered just how much money he made in a year. It had to be significant. Everything about him on the surface screamed wealth. Yet, he wasn't some uppity snob, either. Though we'd gone out to dinner at a posh location, he hadn't put on airs or looked down his nose at anyone.

He'd been a bit of a dork to begin with, but then he'd made jokes and been laidback. I'd had a wonderful time overall. Once we'd gone to the hotel, things went from wonderful to steamy to straight up euphoric. And since I'd watched him choke up at the sonogram visit, I knew he had a more sensitive side to him, too.

While I couldn't forget his reaction to me appearing at his door, he'd asked for forgiveness for that. I'd startled him with my revelation, and he hadn't reacted well. The question was who was Trevor Keller? A nice guy with unorthodox sexual habits or a jerk trying to make nicey-nice for some other hidden purpose?

"Do you have any other children?" I asked next.

"No."

"Ever been married?"

"No."

"Why do you date the way you do?" This time, I held my breath, wondering if he would answer. There are personal questions, and then there are *personal* questions.

"It's simpler. Or, it was," he told me, regarding me with a raised eyebrow. "I discovered long ago that finding a date that is … *compatible* with me can be difficult. So I changed my methods. Knowing what I'm getting into takes out the guesswork. And since I'm not overly fond of guesswork …" He trailed off with a shrug.

Then, he turned the tables. "Okay, your turn. What I know is your full name, that you like *brinner* and eggs in general, and that you're a Zumba instructor. Why don't you fill me in?"

I opened my mouth only to close it again. I wasn't sure how much to divulge. I could handle it if he only wanted the basic statistics, but I didn't think I was ready to share my full tale of woe. That'd likely run him off for good. Maybe if I stuck to the safe topics.

"I was born and raised here in Brooklyn."

"Ah, a true New Yorker," he observed. "So you know all the secrets of the city."

"Don't know about that, but I understand the train conductors a lot better than tourists do. I translate for them sometimes."

He chuckled. "I gotta admit, I rode the dumb thing once and that was enough. I almost missed my stop because I couldn't make heads or tails of any of those announcements."

I laughed, too. I occasionally found dealing with helpless tourists a bit of a hassle, but I was pretty certain if he'd asked me in his charming way, I would've been fine assisting him.

"I'm studying to become a teacher, or I was."

"Was?"

"I dropped out once I discovered I was pregnant."

"Why?" He expression wrinkled as if baffled. "Your college doesn't have some archaic fucked up policy about expectant students or something do they?"

"No." How did I explain this without giving too much away? "I just needed to focus on work."

"Your Zumba?"

"Yeah. And last week I also added some hours as a personal trainer." Lance had come through for me, thank God.

"And then there's your time as an escort," he said, looking away from me as he frowned. But I shook my head.

"That was only a one-time thing."

"That time with me was your first and only time?"

"Yes. Once was more than enough." And not only because of the pregnancy.

He seemed relieved, but then he scrutinized my features as if inspecting me for something I couldn't see. "You never used our safe word. Did I do something that hurt you that night, and you didn't tell me?"

"No." Without thought, I reached out across the table to touch his arm. "I had a lovely time with you."

"But …" His frown deepened. Since he seemed sincerely concerned, I decided to come clean.

"You didn't hurt me. Not at all. I liked it, even the … rougher stuff. Honestly. But I didn't like how it made me feel, the whole getting paid to do it part. So I decided I wouldn't ever do it again."

We grew quiet for a few minutes, each of us digesting what the other had said. Maybe I shouldn't have told him the truth about my time with the Wish Maker, but I didn't want him thinking I was some sort of hooker or whore. I cared about what he thought of me, and if he was of the same opinion as my mother, I couldn't stand that. I took another bite but struggled to get it down. I no longer felt hungry.

"So, teaching, huh?" he broke the silence, and I was glad.

"Yes. Early Childhood."

"How many semesters do you have before you can get your degree?"

Ugh. Just when I thought we'd hit upon an uncomplicated subject. "One."

He frowned. "Okay, you lost me somewhere. Why on God's green planet would you drop out so close to graduation?"

"I told you. So I could work."

"Wait. Is this a money thing?"

Cheese and crackers, I channeled my inner Ashley. I probably should do that anyway so that I didn't curse in front of my innocent child. "I need to save up for the baby."

"But …" He threw up his hands in exasperation, but then seemed to force himself to simmer down. "I guess your education is really none of my business. You've already deferred. But please tell me you'll go back in the fall. I'm here now, and I can help."

"Look, Trevor, that's kind of you, but I like to make my own way. I appreciate you helping to support the baby, but that money won't apply to me. I don't like owing people, and I don't want to owe you."

He blinked at me a few times, but I would stand firm on this. It had taken me years to pay back my debt to those three friends who'd put me up when I was seventeen. It'd ruined those friendships, and I would always regret that.

Only Ashley had remained my friend, and I still owed her big. So big, I didn't know if I'd ever manage to right things between us financially. The difference between her and everyone else was she and her mom loved me, and I loved them. While I was bound and determined to pay them back somehow, I had some wiggle room on the timetable.

But Trevor didn't love me, and I didn't love him. We were already more tangled up than I'd ever planned to be.

Again, there was a prolonged break in our conversation as we both looked anywhere but at each other. Finally, he took the steering wheel again.

"What type of music do you like?" This was from out of the blue, but he was trying so I would, too.

"Hard rock and R & B."

He nodded as if in approval. "Good choices, though in deference to where I'm from, I have to add some Cajun and country to the mix. Favorite type of movie?"

"Action adventure and superhero movies. I'm kinda a nerd."

"What, no chick flicks?" he teased, and his smile peeked at me again. With that scruff on his chin, he was way too handsome for his own good.

"No. I'll watch one with Ashley now and again, but I'm not a huge fan."

"Who's Ashley?"

I hadn't told him about my best friend? "She's my roommate and bestie. She's awesome."

"I'll have to meet her sometime."

"Does that mean I'll meet your friends?"

"Well, all mine are back in Louisiana with my family. Does your family live locally?"

"Ashley and her mom are my family. Her mom lives in California, though." I felt my muscles stiffen up as I waited for him to pry, but he didn't. Thank God for small mercies.

"Oh, almost forgot." He pulled a white paper bag from an inner pocket of his long wool coat and handed it to me. "It's your prenatal vitamins. You told Dr. Carrey you were feeling tired. Besides, you can't fight me on this because right now, your health *is* the baby's health."

Not willing to quibble on such a minor detail, I gave in. "Thank you."

The server brought our bill, which Trevor grabbed with a quick, "No worries, you can get it next time."

I let that go, too. But I *would* pay next time.

There was an uneasy moment once we were back out on the sidewalk together. What was the appropriate protocol for saying goodbye to a man who'd impregnated you while on a paid date, proceeded to call you a liar when you told him about the baby, then seemed to change his mind and get all supportive? I didn't know. As much as I wanted to trust that he had my best interests at heart, it was more likely that he was only coming around because I carried his child.

Great. Now I was being selfish.

I was so up in my head about things that I missed him coming closer to me until his lips landed briefly at my temple.

"Text me where you want to go Friday," he said. Then as he stepped away, he offered me a smile and a wave as he strode off in the opposite direction.

I waved back. Okay, maybe I was overthinking this.

"I will."

14

TREVOR

"How many pieces of baby furniture do you have so far?" I asked Jessica with a slightly raised voice as we sat at a burger place the following week. I suggested the rather noisy family eatery because of a certain item on their menu, a burger with a fried egg on it.

And yes, that's exactly what she'd ordered.

"Including my old dresser which I'm going to clear off to use as a changing station? One."

I chuckled at her joke. "My research shows that you might be in need of a few more."

Her rosebud lips curved up into a smile, her jade eyes sparkling. She looked more energetic today. Less tired. "Research, huh? Are you one of those guys who does research on everything? Like which shampoo get the highest reviews on Amazon?"

"Yes, actually. I'm not a fan of going into something totally blind."

Her smile slipped. "Me either, but I think we're getting ready to have to face it anyway."

"That's not strictly true. I've been looking up everything I can on pregnancy, delivery, and child-rearing. There's a lot of recommendations and empirical data out there, not to mention practical experiences parents have shared. We're both smart, capable people. Between the two of us, I think we'll be able to deal with it."

She raised an arched eyebrow at me. "And here I thought I had the drop on you since I've been reading *What to Expect When You're Expecting*."

"I saw that book on the recommended reading list. I've already downloaded to my Kindle app." At that, she tipped her head back and laughed, her wild curls dancing around her face. Christ, she was so fucking gorgeous. "Why are you laughing?"

"I just find it funny that you're willing to read a book meant for pregnant ladies."

"You're only pregnant because I made you that way. Just trying to do my due diligence before I run out of time."

Her features softened, and she clutched onto my hand where it lay on the table. "That's sweet."

I've been called many things but "sweet" had never been one of them. "I wasn't looking to become a father, Jessica. But now that it's happened, I want to be the best."

"Were you one of those kids who had straight As in school?"

"No. I was more of a jock. I loved playing football, so I kept my grades up enough not to get thrown off the team. Never had a four-point GPA, though. I'd hoped to get a shot to play in college, but I blew out my knee my senior year of high school. So, there went that idea."

"Did it make you sad?" she asked me, her hand still holding mine.

"Eh, at the time I was pretty down. But then, I started taking more of an interest in business. It's served me well. Better than if I'd played pro ball. Though, I do miss being out on that field sometimes." I still found great solace in working out and building up a sweat.

We'd both finished our meals, but I wasn't eager to end our time together. How had this lunch hour gone by so fast?

"Maybe I should turn that question around on you? Were you a straight-A kid?"

"Never, though I did make honor roll a few times. I loved school. It was my sanctuary." She pulled her hand back and fell quiet after this, her expression pensive. I got the impression that she regretted what she'd said. "Better get going. I've got another class in a few minutes."

Reluctantly, I stood, opening the glass door for her on the way out. Over the few glimpses she'd allowed me into her past, I sensed that she had experienced some pretty bad times. I was curious about this, but I hesitated to ask her to go more into depth. If she thought I should know, she'd tell me. Once outside, the noise level dropped, and I was thankful.

"The reason I mentioned supplies was I thought maybe we could go shopping for them together," I suggested. "What do you think?"

"I'd like that. When?"

"Tomorrow?" What I really wanted was to spend the rest of the day with her, even though we both had work. Each of our lunches together had gone well, but they'd left me wanting more. Every time when I'd gone back to my office, I smelled her light scent on my clothes, and I'd had to concentrate hard to regain my focus.

"I have a full day of classes tomorrow."

"Sunday?" I hoped I wasn't coming off as desperate.

"Sure."

"There are a bunch of baby stores listed in DUMBO and Tribeca. Can I pick you up at your place?" I said, mentioning the shorthand for the section of the city otherwise known as Down Under the Manhattan Bridge Overpass.

She hesitated for just a second, then nodded. "Yeah, okay. Here's my address."

∽

Sunday started out cloudy and drizzly, and I was afraid Jessica might cancel on me. What fun would it be to go shopping in such icky weather? But then, just as I pulled up in my SUV, the precipitation tapered off, making the umbrella I'd brought less necessary. I hit the buzzer.

"Yes," came a soprano voice nothing like the mother of my child's.

"This is Trevor. I'm here for Jessica."

"She says you can come on up."

Those words encouraged me. I hadn't expected an invite inside. Swiftly traversing the three flights to her level, I punched the doorbell to apartment 323. A blond woman with pixie-like hair came to the door, her big light blue eyes narrowed in scrutiny.

"Jessie's still getting ready," she said, her pint-sized frame stationed on the threshold like a sentinel. Was she going to let me in?

"Sorry I'm running late," I heard Jessica's disembodied voice from another room. "I overslept. Feel free to come in and have a seat, though."

For a minute, I thought pixie girl wasn't having it. She continued to regard me like she might a mangy rat. But then, she relented, letting me pass. Their abode was clean but spare on room. Unlike many New York apartments, this one was broken up into separate rooms, but instead of making the place more accessible, it only magnified the lack of space.

Pixie girl and I stood in their snug living room. It was only large enough for a loveseat and a flat panel television attached to the wall. Jutting off to my right was a galley kitchen, if you could actually call it that. The thing was so narrow that I wondered if both Jessica and her roommate could be in there at the same time without bumping into each other. Since both were about a size two and around five feet tall, that was saying something.

Off the common areas of the residence were three doors, one of which had been wedged open and was emitting steam —the bathroom—while the other two remained closed. Jessica came out of the bathroom in a terry cloth robe, her hair in a towel. Blood rushed below my belt, and I felt an impulse to rip them both off her so I could see the splendor of her freshly showered flesh underneath. I glanced away from her because I had to.

Guess I needed to increase my own warm shower time.

Luckily, the courtesy and manners that had been drilled into me since birth kicked in automatically. "Nice place you got here."

"Thanks," Jessica called as she hurried into her bedroom. "You want something to drink? We have juice and spring water. Ash, could you get him something?"

Ashley took the two steps required to enter their kitchen. "I'm fine, but thanks," I said, and she disappeared into the other bedroom.

Though their home wasn't spacious, it was tidy and well-kept. I'd anticipated bearing witness to frills and girly stuff, but that wasn't the case. The decorations were fairly sparse, with one garage door like window lighting the living room and framed pictures covering the walls in swaths.

When I scooted closer, I could see that Jessica was in most of them with pixie girl. There was also another woman probably twenty or so years older. Her blond hair and pert nose indicated that she must be the roommate's mother. I pored over these photos and took in a younger version of the mother of my child. In only one of them was she truly smiling. In the rest, she merely offered a shy Mona Lisa style grin.

I knew that grin. It'd been the one she wore once during the dinner portion of our first "date."

There was one particular photo collage that kept drawing my attention, and after glancing at all the others, I went back to it. Jessica appeared to be young—maybe still in high school—as pixie girl wrapped an arm around her shoulders. Jessica had on the Mona Lisa grin, but the grin seemed pained and came off more like a grimace.

I leaned in even closer and studied her striking eyes only to find them utterly devoid of life. It was like looking not at the teenaged Jessica at all, but of a plastic manufactured version of her. A Jessica doll. Despite it being unforgivably nosy, I removed the frame, opened it and inspected the back of the photo.

It said "Ash and Jessie" followed by the date, which was four years ago. I knew I was infringing on her privacy and that I should put it back, but I couldn't. I'd never seen Jessica's features look like this, like she was an empty shell. Like she was dead inside.

I couldn't put my finger on why but seeing her like this was disturbing. Frightening, even. What had happened to leave an expression of such utter despair on her face?

I became so consumed by speculating about this that I didn't have a chance to return the picture to its proper place before Jessica appeared at my side. I glanced over at her, caught red-handed. "What are you doing?"

I replaced the cardboard backing and repositioned it on the nail in the plaster. "Checking out your photo collection."

"Oh." She spoke in a carefully neutral monotone.

"This one is from four years ago. Was it taken while you were in high school?"

"Yes. That was shortly before we graduated." The monotone persisted. I waited for her to elaborate, but she didn't. I was curious as all hell, but I didn't want to push. If she wanted me to know, she'd tell me, right?

Damn, I really wanted her to tell me.

Then, her roommate materialized at her shoulder and handed over a cell phone. "All charged up, honey. You sure you're going to be okay today?"

Her words seemed to bring Jessica back to herself. "Of course, silly. I was just tired."

"If you say so."

"We can delay this," I added. I'd been looking forward to spending this time with Jessica, but if she needed to rest, she should.

"No, I'm good. Let's go."

For the first time, I absorbed what she was wearing. It was different than anything I'd seen her in before, baggier and much, much more threadbare. There was a ruffled shirt that looked frayed along the edges of each ruffle, as well as jeans that had holes in both knees. But the holes didn't appear to be artfully applied as much as worn through the thin fabric. I helped her into her coat but wondered if that'd be enough to keep her warm.

I made a note to look into purchasing some maternity clothes ASAP.

When we went outside, the gray skies had half cleared, allowing a few rays of sunshine to drift down over the city like a soft veil. We crossed over into Manhattan and entered the first infant store I'd ever been in, since I'd bought stuff for Jax's kids online.

It was quite an education, and not just for me, but for Jessica, too. We listened as a sales lady told us all about diaper genies and highchairs, about making our homes child-proof and which toys stimulated an infant brain most effectively.

About an hour in, I asked the lady to give us a moment, and asked Jessica which items she liked. She pointed at a few, bypassing some others, and anything her eyes lit on, I took a quick phone pic of. Then, I waved down our sales lady.

"We'll need two of all these," I said, showing her each item in succession.

"Are these purchases or are you putting them on your baby registry, sir?"

"Purchases," I told her.

"Trevor, may I speak to you? Over here, please?" Jessica led me across the room, the look in her eyes a bit manic.

"What is it? What's wrong?"

"You can't buy all this. Especially not two of each."

"Why not?" I asked her, stymied. "Did you change your mind about something?"

She huffed out a breath as if I caused her some great offense. "One set of what you just picked out is thousands of dollar's worth of merchandise."

"Yeah," I said, still not getting what the problem was.

"And you asked for *two*." Her eyes were huge. Weird.

"Yeah. One set for my apartment and one for yours. We both need a crib and a stroller and so forth. Right?" What was I not seeing here?

"But I can't let you get all this, especially not for my room."

Finally, I thought I understood.

"The baby needs it, and it'll make your life easier. I can afford it, so don't fight me on this, okay?"

"But I don't even know if it'll fit. Ashley traded with me so I could have the bigger bedroom, but it's still not exactly spacious."

"We'll make it work," I told her, but I did need to get a look at her room so I could estimate how cramped things might be in there. "And anything that you might only need occasionally can be kept in a storage space or my place, okay. I know this is a lot, but we'll figure it out."

A line had furrowed deeply into the smooth copper skin between her eyes. She was so cute when she worried over trivialities I was more than happy to take care of. Without conscious thought, I leaned over and kissed that line until it faded into a look of surprise. Then, after giving the sales lady the two separate shipping addresses, we went on to the next store.

After visiting three more stores full of furniture, interactive features like mobiles, and baby clothing, I felt more prepared to welcome our bundle of joy. It occurred to me that I needed to start interviewing nannies as well, since I would still be required to put in just as many hours as usual at the office. In my head, I'd worked out the math that if Jessica and I shared joint custody, I'd need a live-in employee on a full-time basis.

I also needed to discuss this with the woman carrying my child, but so far, it felt too soon. I wasn't certain how such a conversation would go and wasn't in a hurry to start some garish shouting match.

We'd been getting along well, all things considered, and I didn't want to wreck the peace between us. I'd been such an oaf when she'd clotheslined me with the news, and I would never forget that. My bad behavior had created a chasm between us, and now, I was doing my damnedest to make up for it.

I turned at the unexpected sound of Jessica's snort. Since she wasn't one to laugh often, I glanced over to see what she was laughing at. It was a series of something I'd recently learned were called onesies—a one-piece garment that snapped over the infant's diapers.

The first one said, "That awkward moment when your mom sniffs your butt in front of your friends." The one next to it said, "It's all shits and giggles until someone shits and giggles." I chuckled under my breath at the first two, but it was the last one that got my goat for real. "I was Daddy's fastest swimmer."

I laughed so hard heads swiveled in our direction. The fascinating thing was that my outburst sparked Jessica's, and soon we were both nearly rolling in the aisle. I couldn't say what triggered our mutual hilarity. But all I kept picturing was that one tenacious-ass sperm of mine that sped through hell and high water—including a goddamn *condom*—to make this pregnancy happen.

I didn't regain my cool until I realized that I had both my arms around her shoulders, while each of her hands were clinging to my middle for dear life. And even then, cool wasn't what I felt. I peered down at her at the same moment that she peeked up at me, and something shifted somewhere near the region of my ribcage.

It felt like being flung from a merry-go-round already spinning at top speed, yet instead of finding myself bruised on the ground, I felt uplifted. High, even. It was the strangest sensation ever. And the strangest thing of all was it had nothing whatsoever to do with our sexual compatibility. I'd experienced plenty of lust around her, but this wasn't that. This was something else, something I'd never felt before.

I took a step back from her—just a small one—in order to gain some perspective. The instant I broke contact with her, I felt a twinge of absence like ... a loss.

What the hell was that?

Maybe it was that we were having a baby together. That was a connection that would never be broken. No matter what transpired between us going forward, once that child had been brought into the world, I would forever be its father while Jessica was its mother. We would always have that touchstone, that bond. So that high feeling must be that.

Right?

15

JESSIE

APRIL

I stared up at the ceiling. It was after one in the morning, but despite the pall of exhaustion that tended to hang over me, I couldn't make my eyes stay shut. Part of it was because the baby was kicking me, but it was also because I kept reliving the episode I'd shared with Trevor at the baby boutique a few weeks back.

We'd had … a moment. The kind I'd heard about but never experienced. We'd gone from busting a gut to just staring at each other like a couple of sappy imbeciles, and I hadn't known what to make of it.

I still didn't.

That moment had seemed to stretch out and hover there for an indeterminate amount of time as his amber eyes bored into mine. There'd been both intensity and a sense of wonder that had blossomed between us, but I couldn't say what any of it meant. Trevor had been the one to back off, and I'd been glad when he did. Or so I thought. But I kept missing the heat of his arms surrounding me all the way home.

In fact, if I let myself, I could still imagine the heat of them around me now.

Trevor and I continued to hang out together. He went with me to all my prenatal appointments, and our lunch outings increased from twice a week to four or five. We grew closer and developed what I'd have to call a quasi-friendship. I learned that he liked to tell jokes, many of them puns about something sexual. At first, I hadn't known how to react to these, but eventually I accepted that his humor was just of the bawdier sort.

Considering his preferences in the bedroom, I shouldn't have been shocked by this.

But even his dirty sense of humor never strayed into the realm of something disgusting or inappropriate. They were more mischievous than anything else, and lately, I'd found myself snickering at them more often than not. And every time I did, he beamed at me. Not smiled, *beamed*. Like a beacon inside of a lighthouse. I enjoyed seeing his handsome face light up like that. It made his eyes gleam and drew attention to his scruff-covered square jaw.

It was as if he was growing more and more attractive with each passing day. The opposite of what was happening to me. I'd gotten to the point in my pregnancy where I couldn't hide anything. One look from anyone confirmed my condition, and even simple tasks like getting up and down from the loveseat or sliding into and out of a vehicle became much more difficult than I would've previously considered.

I wasn't sure if it was due to this change or not, but Trevor had taken to touching me more. He would rest a palm at the bottom of my spine as I swayed—I no longer merely walked—beside him. He'd take my hand to help me up or down and in or out. Anytime we were caught in a crowd, he stood to one side of me, with one arm around my shoulders and the other over my bulging belly.

If I hadn't been pregnant, such protectiveness might've felt too aggressive or possessive to me, but the solicitous way he stood between me and any possible threat made me feel important. Treasured. Cherished. And no one had ever made me feel that way.

I reasoned that this was simply his response to becoming a father. He was protecting the baby more so than me. But then I started to watch other men with their expectant significant others. Some would show these women no deference at all. There was no door opening or preferential care.

Yet some would do as Trevor would and lavish their women with limitless attention. Most of these men appeared to be married to these women. I saw wedding rings on them ninety percent of the time. They'd also help with any additional children already a part of their families.

I could tell that these couples faced parenthood as a team. And though I'd never say anything to Trevor about my desires other than what I thought the baby might need, I wanted what these couples had. The unity. The commitment. The trust. The love.

Which was stupid. I would never have all that. If even my mother couldn't love me, how could I expect to ever find a partner who would?

So I went about my days feeling grateful for every fleeting touch Trevor offered me, memorizing every detail. Once this pregnancy was over, all that would end, so I did my best to enjoy his kindness while it lasted.

At seven months along, teaching my Zumba class was becoming a challenge. While I could still do all the moves necessary, my stamina had taken a hit, and I struggled to complete each hour-long session. One day Trevor sauntered in just prior to the cool down exercises and found me sweating profusely at the front. Normally, by the time I saw him for our lunches, I'd showered and cleaned up, but this time he caught me early.

Redoubling my efforts to look strong as I finished, I dug deep and completed the set with more vigor than I really felt. Unfortunately, this meant I was shaky by the end, a fact I attempted to conceal from him as he approached.

"Are you all right?" he asked me, his voice edged with worry.

Okay, so epic fail on the "I might be knocked up, but you will still hear me roar" front.

"Yeah," I told him, huffing and puffing. That should help my case. *Not*. "Just ... just about to jump in the shower."

"You look like you're about to fall over, Jessica. Sit down."

I bristled at this. He had no right to order me around. I continued to stand out of sheer defiance. "Stop it, Trevor. I'm fine."

"You're pale and shaking like a leaf," he countered, crossing his arms over his broad chest.

"No, I'm not," I argued, even though what he said was undeniable.

"Have you eaten today?" This came out as a terse demand for answers, and I pursed my lips at him. He was pissing me off.

"Yes, I had a …" But when I thought about it, I had to backtrack. I hadn't felt hungry this morning and had skipped breakfast. I used to do it all the time before I was pregnant, so it shouldn't matter, should it? Yet, I did feel a little woozy. Not that I'd mention that to him. Time to change tack. "Why are you here so early anyway?"

"Your checkup. It's at noon, remember?"

Shit. No, I hadn't remembered. *Cheese and crackers.* Maybe this stuff I'd been hearing about pregnancy brain really was a thing.

"Um …" was my ever-so-witty comeback. He yanked at his phone with the short jerky movements I'd come to recognize as his aggravated mood, scrolling through his contacts. "What are you doing?" I asked him.

"I'm rescheduling. I need to get you something to eat."

"No," I protested, grabbing at his cell even though I shouldn't. "We're going to find out the gender today."

He'd been contemplating the screen of his phone, but now, he squinted at me. "That can wait. You need food more than you need to know about the sex."

A vein in his neck was popping out a little, so I knew his attitude hadn't improved. That, plus his mention of the word sex, even though it hadn't nothing to do with the act, had thrummed up my body like a struck chord. I ignored it. Or tried to. "What I need is a shower."

"No. If I let you go in there in your current state, you might fall. At least tell me you're hydrated. You've been drinking your water like you're supposed to, right?"

The thing of it was, I hadn't been thirsty, either. Not till now. At that moment, I felt as if I could've drained a camel. Letting myself get to that point had been cardinally dumb. I knew better, but I'd just rushed around and forgotten all about it. Not that I'd admit that to the guy who was chastising me like a recalcitrant toddler, though.

"*Jessica,*" His voice was all warning, so I fired back at him.

"*Trevor.*"

He chuffed out an angry sigh, looked away from me and lifted his phone to his ear once more. "Yes, this is Trevor Keller. Jessie Souza had an appointment at noon but may not be able to make it. Do you have any openings for later today?"

I seized his elbow, but his greater height and strength made my physical challenge more of a symbol of my irritation than anything else. Still, I pinched his bicep for all I was worth and saw him flinch. He didn't spin away from me as I anticipated but kept himself stationary, despite the punishment I inflicted on him.

Mule.

"A cancellation?" he spoke in an unaffected voice. Apparently, what I was doing didn't ruffle him nearly as much as I wanted it to. "2:30pm? We can make that no problem. Thanks so much." He disconnected.

I was so mad at him right then I could've kicked his shin.

I considered it. But then he zeroed in on me again, and I froze. His eyes were ablaze with molten fire, the amber darkening to a deep topaz. Not since our so-called date had I seen such naked desire written all over him, and even that had been the briefest of glimpses before he'd tied a blindfold over my eyes. There was no blindfold now, though, and I felt an answering call, primal and uncontrollable as my panties dampened without my permission.

"Don't start something you can't finish," he ground out, ogling my form up and down as if he wanted to devour me alive.

I hadn't thought such a look was possible. I was hugely pregnant and getting huger all the time. Could he truly want me right now? But even as the question entered my mind, the heat in his answering gaze showed me in no uncertain terms that he wouldn't hesitate to ravish me given the chance.

Holy crap!

He drew a finger along my jaw and down my chin, raising it as he lowered his lips toward mine. I couldn't believe this was happening, and even more, I couldn't believe how much I *yearned* for it to happen.

"Hey, Jessie, I was wondering if I could—Oh!"

Trevor and I snapped out heads up to see my boss Lance sticking his nose into the room. The look on his face might've been comical had he not had the power to rob me of all my sources of income in one fell swoop. He was my direct supervisor for both my instructor position and my fitness trainer job, and if he so chose, he could can me for cavorting on the clock.

"We were just on our way out," Trevor said into the tense silence.

"Uh, I need to go over your most recent group of evaluations," Lance said to me. We were evaluated every six months by both our students and our supervisors, but right now, evaluations were the last thing I could think about.

"Lance, this is Trevor," I made hasty introductions, my voice too high. "Trevor, this is Lance, my boss."

"Lance, those evaluations are going to have to be postponed," Trevor told him, one of his large hands cupping my stomach. "She has a doctor's appointment."

My boss's features went stony, but all he said was a long and drawn out, "Yeah ... Okay."

Trevor stayed by my side until we'd made it to the sidewalk, his posture rigid. "How is he with you?"

"Excuse me?" I asked him, not understanding.

"You're boss. How is he with you? Does he treat you fairly, or does he give you shit?"

"He's fine."

I wouldn't say anything about how Lance had cut my hours a few months ago, because he'd given them back to me when another instructor quit. I think the opening up of my availability had something to do with it, too. I wondered if Lance had planned to tell me to stop due to the pregnancy. I hoped not. I needed to work right up to delivery if possible. I would miss hours once the baby was born as it was.

"Would you tell me if he wasn't?"

Damn, was I that transparent? Feeling a bit gun shy, I gazed up into the face of the father of my child. I didn't see heat or irritation this time. This time there was nothing there but the concern I'd come to know so well.

"I need to stay on good terms with him," I said. "For the sake of my job."

Trevor examined my gaze like he might in a suspense or thriller novel. "You still want a shower?"

"That's a non-negotiable."

"I'm guessing you don't want to take it here."

"No. I'll take one at home."

"I'll drive you," he insisted, and as a wave of drowsiness made me yawn, I gave in.

∼

Dr. Carrey greeted us, as always, with a polite, professional expression. I wondered if they taught physicians how to do that in medical school, maybe under the heading of "bedside manner."

"How are you feeling today, Jessie?"

Trevor had bought me a bottle of water at the gym, driven me home, and waited for me to take a shower. Then he'd taken me by a fresh foods restaurant where we ate raw veggies with hummus and shared a good-sized bowl of nuts mixed with chopped pieces of fruit. He also bought me two additional bottles of water and watched as I drank them down with the meal. I'd felt like grumbling at him the entire time and almost did.

I wasn't going to admit it to him, but I felt significantly better after eating and rehydrating.

"Good," I told my OBGYN.

"Still anxious to determine whether the balloons will be pink or blue?"

"Definitely," Trevor and I said in unison, but I still refused to look at him. I hadn't appreciated his take charge behavior from earlier. I was tempted to tell him that I might've gone along with him being the boss in the bedroom but that didn't mean he got to be that way outside of it. He'd really gotten on my last nerve today, while also turning me on when I didn't want to be.

Jerk.

"You couldn't tell last time," Trevor chimed in, never one to hold back any questions. "What if the same thing happens again?"

"Well, the truth is, sometimes even when we do get a good view of what's between the legs, it can be difficult to determine the gender. That early on everything is still developing and often a penis and clitoris look very much the same."

I wondered if Trevor was stifling all the puns or dirty jokes that had probably started to ping through his brain like popcorn at that little morsel of information.

"Now, however," Dr. Carrey went on, "those parts of the body should be more identifiable. And if they aren't, or if we run into a similar issue as last time, we'll simply run a blood test and find out that way. Any other questions before we do another scan?"

"The baby kicks a lot when I'm trying to sleep but sometimes won't do anything when I'm awake," I told her, casting a sideways glimpse at Trevor. This had been annoying him for a few weeks because not once had he felt the movement of his own child. At first, he'd played it off, but lately, I'd seen unmistakable pain in his eyes over it. Especially when I encouraged the baby to move to no avail. I'd literally said, "Come on, kick for your daddy!"

It hadn't worked.

And as much as I still felt aggravated by his actions this morning, noticing that disappointed look on his face killed me.

"Well," my OBGYN began. "At twenty-eight weeks, it's normal to have periods of rest and periods of activity. Often those are opposite of yours."

Trevor seemed to find one of the posters on the wall fascinating, so I knew this was bothering him. "Is there anything we can do to make the baby kick at a certain time?"

"Talking directly to your stomach usually works. It may sound silly, but the more the baby hears yours and Trevor's voices, the more likely it is to respond to you both."

The father of my child looked back at me, then, his amber eyes more hopeful. As soon as we had a moment alone, I'd encourage him to speak to the baby.

"Let's get you all hooked up," Dr. Carrey said, proceeding with this second scan.

The most beautiful sound in the world filled the room again as she drew the wand across my abdomen. An image filled the screen, and there it was, our baby, its heartbeat going strong. I could listen to that noise and stare at that screen forever. As we all watched, it moved its arm.

"Is it ... is it sucking its thumb?" Trevor asked, his tone one hundred percent awe.

"Sure is. Let's try to go for the money shot again, shall we?"

Dr. Carrey directed the wand over to my left side, and maybe due to this, the baby twisted as if doing a head over heels spin.

"Stop," I whispered out, as if sneaking into a church service late. "Can you take away the wand for a sec?"

My doctor blinked but did as I asked. I flattened my palm to my left side and pressed Trevor's palm to the same spot. "That. That right there. You feel it?"

His amber eyes went from awe to absolute joy as that beaming smile of his filled his face. "Holy shit! Oh my *God*."

"I know, right?" I said, half giggling the words, but I couldn't help it. Trevor's joy was catching.

"Hey, there, kiddo. I'm your daddy." The amazing thing was that the baby kicked harder at the sound of his voice. I was so happy for him, and when his eyes grew overly shiny, mine got all teary, too.

My OBGYN was grinning at us. "Shall we go on with the program?"

"Please," I told her.

She resumed scanning my belly until our baby's bottom was once again on display. This time, though, its legs were spread out into a wide V, giving us a much more definitive view. She froze the frame and took a picture, then she announced the verdict.

"Congratulations. It's a boy."

16

TREVOR

"Congratulations. It's a boy."

The woman's words echoed in the examination room, and I let them wash over me like rain. A boy. A boy. We were having a son. I was smiling so big I thought my face might crack, but I didn't care. The baby was a boy.

A *boy*!

I put my hand back on Jessica's stomach, and even though our son—*our son*—had quit doing somersaults like a gymnast in training so I could no longer feel like tiny thumping against my palm, I didn't move it. This was the best moment of my life, bar none. I couldn't imagine anything being better or more exciting than this. Nothing. I felt giddy. Gleeful. Jubilant.

Jesus Christ.

The doctor had left us alone in the room, but before doing so, she'd frozen the image of our son's teeny-weeny ass on the screen so there could be no doubt. An appendage thrust out from between his legs as clear as day, and even though I'd decided I'd be thrilled either way, knowing it was a boy just made me want to climb to the top of the Empire State Building and bellow out my news for the entire country to hear.

I pictured what it'd be like to put him in pads and a helmet for his first football practice, just like I'd done. I could see him running, throwing the ball, and making a touchdown. I could see him both here in the Big Apple jumping in puddles in Central Park and back at home in the Big Easy, trying barbecue for the first time. There was so much to share. So much I'd get to watch him do. And then, my imagination took another turn, and Jessica was there, as well.

She was there as I handed our son his first football, plush when he was little, then maybe a nerf one before going to the real thing. She was there at his practices and cheering him on as he outran the other team. She was there laughing at his antics as he splashed in those puddles, and she was there in New Orleans, trying Louisiana barbecue, too. She was there with him; with me. We were an *us*. We three, together and happy.

Whoa, was that possible?

And as soon as the query flew through my mind, I knew what I wanted the answer to be.

Yes. Yes, please.

Today had been a study of extremes. Jessica and I had been sniping at each other. She hadn't been taking care of herself and it showed. It pissed me off, and it worried me, not only because of our son, but also because of her. I wanted her healthy not only so she could give me a healthy child, but also for her own sake.

Her expression now was pure elation. And I'm sure mine was, too. It felt like we'd been riding a roller coaster into a roaring tornado ever since this whole thing started. Yet, I couldn't complain.

We were having a boy.

I loved my son with a boundlessness I couldn't even explain. Yet, I felt things for Jessica, as well. I cared about her and wanted her in my future.

So what did that mean?

My brain was too scattered to make sense of what anything meant right now.

All that mattered was that we were going to have a son. A bouncing baby boy. My cheeks began to hurt, and I couldn't care less. It just felt so, so good.

The doctor removed the scanning device from Jessica's belly. As the mother of my son lowered her loose-fitting maternity shirt back into place, I felt an impulse to lug her into my arms and parade around the room with her like an insane person. Instead, I led her out of Womancare and into my SUV.

"Want to come over to my place?" I asked her, visualizing us nestled together on my L-shaped sectional eating takeout Chinese. I also had a massive monitor on my desktop computer where we could sit side by side and pick out some new clothes for the baby. A football uniform—that was a given. And maybe some tiny little jeans and a t-shirt in Saints colors. Maybe one mentioning King Cake or featuring a fleur-de-lis.

"I have a fitness client in about an hour," she said, and for the first time in several minutes, her smile faded. I hated to see that. I would've liked for her smile to be permanent. "And don't you have to get back to work, too?"

Work. I'd totally forgotten about work. Every moment I wasn't either sleeping or spending with Jessica was consumed by investments and tracking down fresh and wealthier clients. Yet, the second I'd heard I was going to be the father of a son, all that had flown out the window like a flock of pigeons.

Whoa.

"You're right. I just ... I guess my mind's been blown."

Her smile came back. "What was it like feeling him bounding around in there? Our baby boy?"

"It was ..." I kept having difficulty formulating coherent sentences. "It was amazing. *You* are amazing."

She glanced down at her hand as it rested on her baby bump, her smile remaining in place. Jessica was glowing. Her black curls surrounded her head like a halo, and her copper skin no longer looked pale. Her jade green eyes, still the slightest bit red around the rims, were sparkling now. I found everything about her to be stunning, just like she had been the first time I'd seen her.

Only this time, it was even better. Her belly was swollen with my child. Her breasts, which had already probably been D cups, had filled out even more beneath her clothing, tantalizing me with their fullness. Her hips were rounder, and the skin of her hands seemed softer. I wondered if her rosebud lips were as supple and pliant as I remembered.

Her reedy-voiced boss had interrupted us earlier, but Lance was nowhere in sight now. We were in my Lexus and hadn't yet pulled out into traffic.

It was as good a time as ever.

So, I twisted, wove my hands into that riotous hair of hers, and took her mouth, sealing my lips over hers. And again, I was arrested by the taste of her, by the sweetness of it. Just like months ago, I felt an almost overwhelming craving to abandon all my control and lose myself in her.

But this time, I didn't yearn to tie her up or to bang her into the bed. This time, I wanted to touch her with just the tips of my fingers, to cuddle and caress her. This time, I wanted to witness her pleasure by gazing into her eyes the moment she came.

I felt the edge of my lust, but I also felt something else. Something different. Whether due to my son growing inside of her or something else, I realized I didn't want to command her to do anything. I didn't want to take the chance that I might harm her, even accidentally. So, I didn't want to dominate her and make her submit. I didn't want any of the trappings my sexual exploits typically required. I didn't want to fuck her.

I wanted to take her in my arms and *make love* to her.

Okay. That was new.

Or maybe it wasn't. Over these past few weeks, we'd been in each other's company frequently. We'd eaten together nearly every day. We'd gone shopping for our son. We'd gone together to her doctor's appointments every single time, and a couple of those times required me to stand near her head because of the intimate nature of those checks. But Jessica had asked me to stay, even when I'd offered to step outside.

We'd become something more, though I didn't know how to label it.

I'd never been someone who apologized for who I am. I accepted long ago that my predilections fell outside what most would probably consider the norm, sexually speaking. Not that I was anything that out there. I'd once gone to a BDSM convention and witnessed some visuals there I'll never be able to forget, some of which turned me on a little and some of which out-and-out repulsed me.

But I'd never been in a place to judge anyone else about what they liked or didn't like, so I never had. Yet, now, I questioned what I'd been doing all this time. When I'd been a teenager and taking my initial forays into physical pleasure with a girl, I'd found myself pushing the traditional envelope right past its limits. None of the girls I'd dated had enjoyed my form of play. Not one.

So, in college, when a friend had mentioned the Wish Maker, I'd started down the path of paying women to be my submissives. That way, I received precisely what I wanted without hesitation or regret.

Never once had I felt bad about anything I'd done to these women. I'd never mistreated them, and I knew I wouldn't see them again. It'd always been a one and done deal for me. I wanted no attachments or entanglements. I wasn't interested in anything with them beyond a night of pleasure.

Yet with Jessica, all that had changed forever.

While she was the most captivatingly stunning woman I'd ever seen on the outside, what I'd become aware of more and more was her beauty on the inside. Though I didn't know all the details, this was a girl who had been beaten up by life. Yet, she hadn't let that thwart her. She had a determination and resilience about her that I admired. Despite her pregnancy affecting the way she moved, she continued to push forward with her two very physical jobs, anyway.

I had to respect her fortitude, and I did.

The trick was that she made me take a closer look at myself. I'd never felt bad for my lifestyle. I'd been focused on my career, and that was fine with me. Or, it had been. Now, being around Jessica so much made me wonder what ever happened to those women I'd fucked halfway into the mattress and then got up and left behind.

Those women were almost caricatures of themselves to me, not real. While I remembered all of them, it was in the same way you might remember a nice collection of paintings in an art museum. I oohed and ahhed, and then, I moved on.

And then Jessica came along. When she'd told me she'd never have sex for money again, I thought I'd understood. I assumed she must've had some sort of moral or ethical reason to stop, which was fine. I'd always been the kind of person to say to each his or her own. But now when I thought of her never sleeping with anyone for money again, I was relieved. Immensely.

Not only because she was having my baby, either, though that was certainly a contributing factor. When I thought about another man being with her sexually—whether for money or not— it made me want to punch something, preferably him. Now, when I thought of how I'd been with her that night, I felt bile rise up my throat like battery acid.

I'd not only treated all my former conquests like objects, I'd treated the *mother of my son* like an object. Like a plaything. Like a sex toy rather like a living breathing woman with a mind, heart, and soul.

And for the first time in my life, I felt ashamed of my love life. Or more correctly, my lack of one. Maybe I'd been fooling myself all along, saying that it was okay because it was just sex. No one was getting hurt. No one was doing anything beyond anyone else's permission. It was all consensual. But Jessica had only been with me that night because she'd needed a decent sized sum of money fast. Which basically meant she'd been desperate.

And I'd been the asshole to use that desperation for my own pleasure.

It didn't matter that she'd received her own pleasure or that I hadn't known her circumstances at the time. It didn't even matter that I didn't know everything about her now. I thought I'd treated her well when I actually hadn't. And that realization made me feel shallow and callous.

Somehow, I'd spent my entire adult life as an arrogant asshole without being conscious of that. Which must mean I was deaf, dumb, and blind when it came to putting other's needs ahead of my own.

I'd always been that way. When Jax had been sent away to London, I'd missed him, sure. But I'd also all too willingly filled in for him, hoping to impress his father. When an opportunity to leave everyone I held dear had arisen, I hadn't hesitated to move states away. I'd leapt at the chance without regard for anything or anyone else.

Looking back at the decisions I made, I didn't feel good about myself. And though kissing Jessica was one of my favorite activities ever, I broke the seal of our lips and sat back. Averting my eyes, I peered out at the hustle and bustle surrounding us. The city had transitioned into spring, the leaves had already gone from buds to leaves. The bare branches had filled with vibrant green as New York had blossomed into view.

Just like my son would be doing in a couple of months.

Jesus Christ, if there was ever a time to get my shit together, it was now.

"Trevor," Jessica brought my attention back to her sublime face. "Are you okay?"

"S-sure … uh …" God, I was stuttering. What the ever-loving hell? "Just really excited, you know?"

"Okay." She lifted one delicately arched eyebrow. "But you seem kinda freaked out."

"N-no," Still stammering. Awesome. "No, I just need to get to work, like you said. How about I take you out to dinner tonight to celebrate? We can go to a movie, too, if you want."

She patted her belly. "Don't know if my bladder could handle a movie."

"Well, we'll head to my place instead, then. We can watch one there. If I don't already have the movie you want, I'll either stream one or download it digitally."

There. Hopefully that smoothed things over. At least I'd gotten past sounding like Daffy fucking Duck.

"I'd like that."

"Cool," I told her, hazarding a brief glance without holding her gaze. "Let me drop you at the gym, and I'll come get you at your place at eight."

Then, I flipped on Sirius Radio to fill the car with music, negating the need to fill the SUV with any more talk. I needed to process my thoughts, to figure out how to be what Jessica and my son needed me to be.

17

JESSIE

Hearing that our baby was a boy created a bubble of happiness inside me. Seeing that one identifying feature on the sonogram today and sharing that with Trevor meant so much to me. We were having a son, a baby boy that would be half him and half me. It brought the reality of this child and my love for him into sharp focus. It made me want to go out and buy a bib featuring a bow tie.

I couldn't wait to tell Ashley.

And Trevor asked me out tonight, too. Not just out to lunch like we'd done so many times, but out to dinner. Maybe the time of day we'd be eating together shouldn't alter its significance so much, but it did. Dinner implied something more serious. Something more ... romantic. Or at least, it could. I didn't want to read more into it than there was, but still.

Trevor and I hadn't had dinner together since this baby's conception. It just felt like more of a big deal.

And though I hadn't admitted this to myself before, I wanted it to be.

Something about all our recent interactions had brought my feelings for Trevor to the fore. At first, I'd just ascribed it to physical attraction and hormones. I mean, our first night together had been damn near explosive. I'd had a handful of partners, but no one had made me soar like Trevor had.

Then, at the gym, he'd kissed me. It'd been such a searing kiss, too. One I'd been in danger of losing myself in, despite the fact that we'd been at my workplace. I'd never been like that before with anyone else. PDA was not my normal MO. Yet, I hadn't cared. And tonight, we had more plans.

But was it just me, or had he seemed a little off right before he'd dropped me back at work?

Pushing that idea out of my mind, I texted my BFF.

Guess what.

What? She sent back.

It's a boy.

A BOY! YAY! SCREAMING AND HOLLERING AND THROWING CONFETTI RIGHT HERE IN CLASS!

I giggled like a little girl, glad my fitness client hadn't arrived yet. Then, when he showed up, I did my best to sedately lead him through a rotation on the weight machines.

∼

After getting home I went straight to the shower so I could get ready for my dinner date. Ashley popped into the room and spoke to me through the shower curtain.

"A BOY!" she shrieked, and after I came back to life from the heart attack she'd caused me, I peeked out at her.

"A boy," I echoed, grinning from ear to ear.

"Have you guys been thinking about names?"

"Maybe a few, though we haven't mentioned any to each other."

"Well, I have a few," she said, her tone impish.

"Let's hear 'em.'

"How about Rupert?"

"*Rupert*? Really?" I asked her.

"No? Nigel, then."

I snorted. "That one's even worse."

"Miles?"

"That sounds like a butler, and I just don't want to limit his choices like that."

This time it was Ashley who snorted. "Bernard."

"Maybe once he turns eighty."

"You're totally bogarting all my suggestions."

"All your suggestions are bizarre," I countered. "Are you going to name your kids any of these once it's your turn?"

"Absolutely. Those names are classy."

"Those names are archaic," I quipped back, and that time we both dissolved into snickers. It took a few minutes before we sobered, and I dried off. Once done, she handed me my robe, but my tummy now protruded out of it. We went to my room where I started to pick through my wet hair, and a conclusion I'd recently come to burst out of me of its own accord. "Ash?"

"Uh huh."

"I think I have a thing for Trevor."

"A thing?" She plopped on my bed, seizing my pillow to lean on.

"Yeah."

"Like an attraction thing? A fascination thing? An obsessive-compulsive thing? What kind of thing are we talking about here?"

"A uh … *love* thing," I clarified. Saying the word out loud gave it a certain impetus, like I'd released a genie from its bottle and didn't know what it might do.

"Oh." Ashley went exceptionally quiet after that, staring down at her cuticles.

"You're not saying anything."

"No. No, I'm not."

That wasn't a good sign. "Why not?"

"Because you have that hopeful look in your eye, and I don't want it to go away."

"You don't think we'll work out."

"I think you're in a difficult situation. You're looking at either raising little Dougal all by your lonesome—with help from me, of course. Or, if you were to get with Trevor, you'd be a team. A mommy and daddy together. It makes sense to want that, even if it might be a marriage of convenience."

"Marriage?" I blew out a gust of air. "Who said anything about marriage?"

"It's a figure of speech," she said, waving me off.

"This wouldn't be about marriage, probably. It's just that I... love him."

She went still as a statue in response.

"What's wrong with that?" I demanded of her.

"Nothing, if you don't mind getting your heart broken." Then, she winced at the same time I did. "I'm not trying to bring you down, honey, but look at the facts. He's a rich powerful businessman in his prime. You went on a paid date with him that wound up producing a child. There's just so many cards stacked against you."

"We're getting to know each other," I argued.

"So he knows about your first pregnancy?"

"He knows I had a prior miscarriage, yes."

"So he knows who was responsible and how it happened? The horror and pain you went through?" she whispered as if saying those words quietly would lessen their impact. It didn't.

"No," I mumbled.

"Or what your mother did in response?"

"No," I mouthed.

Trevor knew next to nothing about my past. Not only because it was hard to talk about, but also because I couldn't imagine any man wanting me after finding out something like that. What guy would want a girl who'd been both broken beyond repair and rejected by the only family she'd ever had?

Ashley stood, grabbed my wrist, and brought over to the mattress to sit beside her. "I'm not saying this to be hurtful, honey. I'm saying this because these are all things a man you might want to build a relationship with needs to know. These are secrets that you've been hiding, but if you plan on trying something real with him, you'll have to be more honest and open about this stuff."

"What if I explain it all and he heads for the hills?"

"That would suck," Ashley said. "But at least then you'd know if he was in it for the long haul."

I rested my head on her shoulder, considering what she'd said. My best friend always had my best interests at heart, so I knew that listening to her was a wise decision. I'd need to think about this.

"Ash?"

"Yeah?"

"Dougal's out, too."

She sighed.

~

At seven that evening, I put on the only maternity dress I had, a black cotton number that Trevor had bought me. I'd refused to accept it at first, saying he didn't need to purchase clothing for me, but he'd said it was a late Christmas gift so I had to take it.

I'd also wiggled into some ballet flats that used to belong to Ashley's mom. My feet had swollen too big to wear the only other pair of flats I owned. At seven thirty, I began to apply a few touches of makeup. At a quarter till, I was ready. And one minute later, Trevor set off the door buzzer.

"I'll come down to you," I told him.

"No, I'll come up. Wait for me."

When Trevor appeared, he wore jeans, low cut leather boots, and a Henley. That casual appearance agreed with him in spectacular fashion. He looked good enough to eat, despite that not being the plan. I gave myself an internal headshake. This whole being with child thing had wreaked so much havoc on my hormones that I literally ached for his touch sometimes.

Not that he knew that.

And I wasn't about to ask for a pity lay. That would just be pathetic.

I greeted him, but he said nothing back. He also seemed a bit pale now that I looked more closely at him, as if under the weather. I cocked my head to the side as I studied him, but as if coming back from somewhere scary and far away, he refocused on me and held out his arm.

"Your chariot awaits, m'lady."

"Wow. That was super cheesy."

Finally, his lips quirked upward into a smile. "There's more where that came from, but like a contestant on Jeopardy, I thought I'd phrase them in the form of a question."

"Oh, yeah? Lay 'em on me. But you have to answer the same questions for yourself."

"I'm good with that."

As he led me down my three flights of stairs as if I were some fragile china doll, he began his silly game.

"Hey, baby, what's your sign?" he affected a voice I could only describe as greasy used car salesman.

I snickered at him. It was so bad I couldn't help myself. "I'm a Leo."

"Aquarius," he said. "Favorite color?"

"Green."

"Blue for me. And speaking of blue, is that the color you're painting your room for the baby?"

"No. We're not allowed to paint since we're renting."

"I'm going to paint mine. I was thinking of turning my second bedroom into the nursery. I've just got to take out my treadmill and weight set and stow it in my home office."

How often did he expect our son to be with him? The inquiry was on the tip of my tongue, but I didn't ask him. Suddenly, I felt too hot and felt glad to traipse out into the night air. The sounds of Brooklyn rushed at us, the cars honking, the sirens wailing, the music of a passing vehicle blaring. It was a welcome interruption. We continued our game as Trevor left the streets I'd grown up on to head across town.

"Where are you taking me, anyway?"

"Claw Daddy's."

"Claw … what?"

He chuckled. "Claw Daddy's. It's a Cajun and Creole place over on Orchard Street in the East Village. I feel like you and I are doing this gigantically momentous thing together, but there's still things we don't know about each other. So, I thought I'd let you experience the food often boiling in my nana's kitchen when I was a kid."

A warmth I hadn't seen coming filled my chest. The way he spoke about his nana made it obvious that he loved her. "Your nana sounds like a neat lady."

"She was the best. I'd come home from school and steam would be rising from her pots on the stove. The smell of butter and crawdads is the best ever created."

I couldn't help but notice he'd used the past tense when describing her.

"I hope this place is up to scratch," he went on, and if I wasn't mistaken, a certain twang had entered his speech. "I haven't tried it before. The pictures on Yelp look pretty inviting, though. It probably wouldn't be quite up to Nana's standards, but then again, nothing ever was."

"Do you ever get homesick being so far away from your hometown?"

"Sometimes," he said, sounding contemplative. The lights curving over the Williamsburg Bridge flickered across him as we crossed the East River, throwing his hands on the steering wheel into alternating bands of lightness and darkness like an old movie reel. "Mostly, I'm too busy to worry about it much."

His unconcerned words contradicted the sorrow in his voice, though.

"How about your nana? Do you miss her?" I held my breath when I mentioned his nana. It felt risqué to go there.

"Every single day. She died five years ago, right after I turned twenty. She was a tough old bird and lived all the way to ninety." His features were a mix of sadness and fond remembrance. "The folks and I got along okay, but they're foreign diplomats who traveled all the time. Still do. I hardly ever saw them then or now. Nana is my dad's mama. She's the one who really raised me."

"I'm sorry for your loss."

"Nah, I'm fine. You gotta grow up sometime. My only regret was that she'll never see our son, you know?"

My eyes grew hot and began to sting. Time to change subjects. "Have you been thinking about any names?"

"Don't hate me, but no. Not yet, anyway."

"I don't hate you, but be forewarned, Ashley has made it her life's mission to name him something ancient-sounding."

"Ancient-sounding?" he huffed out a chuckle.

"Yes. So far she's mentioned Dougal, Bernard, Miles, Nigel, and Rupert. All of which I adamantly vetoed."

He laughed louder then. "Those are ... interesting."

"No, they're not. They're horrible. You don't have to be diplomatic."

"Those sound distinctly British to me. Does she have that kind of ancestry or something?"

"I don't know. Maybe. She loves the UK, I know that. England, Wales, Scotland, and Ireland are all on her bucket list, but she's never been out of the country."

"Not even to Mexico or Canada?"

"Afraid not."

"Before I turned ten, my parents did the 'travel with your kid' thing. I remember being in all these far-flung places, some of which were dangerous for Americans. Finally, Nana put her foot down and insisted I stay with her. I was a much happier camper after that."

"How many countries did you visit?" I didn't think I could even imagine such an existence.

"Oh, damn. Let's see ... There was Russia, China, France, Japan, Turkey, Germany, and Brazil. I may be forgetting a few, but they all kind of blurred together at a certain point.

Since I was a kid, the main thing I cared about was if there were sweets and whether other children my age were around to play with. In Brazil I wandered off into the forest and had to hide from what I later realized were likely members of the local drug cartel. That was my last trip."

"God, Trevor. It's a wonder nothing terrible happened to you." My heart pounded with fear despite him being safe and sound next to me.

"I know." My brain was still reeling from this shocking piece of information when he switched topics. "Have you ever had crawfish etouffee?"

I'd never even heard of etouffee, whatever that was. "No."

"You've gotta try it. It can be spicy, but I think you'll enjoy it. How about a po' boy sandwich?"

"I once tried a shrimp po' boy during a Mardi Gras festival we had at school. It was good."

He nodded. "Have you ever attended Mardi Gras?"

"No. Never been out of New York."

"The state?" he sounded incredulous.

"The city."

He glanced at me with wide eyes at that news. "Seriously?"

"Seriously." That's me. Ms. Never Go Anywhere. If the destination wasn't on my MetroCard, it probably meant I hadn't been there.

"I'll have to remedy that at some point."

As Trevor escorted me inside, the noise level was high. It was one of those restaurants where people came to knock back a few beers and relax with friends, family, or coworkers. Nearly every table had four or more people surrounding it, some of them wearing plastic bibs, and the décor was simple, with wooden chairs, laminate tables, and paper towels right at the center.

The scent of freshly cooked seafood drifted over to us, and immediately my stomach moved. Apparently, our son had similar tastes to his father. Chalkboards filled out large sections of each wall advertising happy hour and the specials of the day. Fishing nets serving as lighting fixtures hung from the ceiling overhead, adding another touch of authenticity.

The meal turned out to be excellent. I had corn on the cob, crawfish, and snow crab legs while Trevor had clams and lobster served with a sauce so spicy it was literally entitled "Insane" on the menu. We tried each other's meals, though I took only a teeny bite of his. It was way too high on the Scoville scale for me. I had to down a full glass of water afterwards.

Trevor bit his cheek as if to keep from laughing at me, but I nearly kicked him anyway. I wondered if his nana had been in the circus as a freaking fire-eater. He seemed to have a good time there, coming across as more relaxed than I'd ever seen him. And when I asked him how it compared to his nana's he said the following:

"Not as good, but not bad."

We both ate enough to have us groaning, and I joked that I needed a dump truck to haul me to his SUV. We stayed in physical contact throughout our dinner, which he referred to as "supper." Trevor's hand remained on my shoulder, my arm, or my hand. We feed each other and then cleaned one another up with the paper towels provided. And when I told him about the baby leaping around in reaction to the food, he rubbed my stomach while wearing a massive grin.

"That's my boy."

When I begged off of dessert, he ordered some lava cake despite this, telling me we could have it later at his place. For some reason, his mention of going back to his apartment sent a thrill up my spine.

I'd been there before, but not only had that meeting gone badly, I'd only seen what amounted to his entryway. Him bringing me there now seemed to cement something together that had been separate up till now, and I felt equal parts nerves and anticipation as we headed toward that section of the city.

"Home sweet home," he said as we entered, lights coming on automatically as he crossed into each room.

I watched as he put away the brown bag with the dessert into his bright stainless-steel fridge. I couldn't help but ogle at his place. It was ten times bigger than what Ashley and I called our quaint and cozy hole in the wall in Brooklyn. His kitchen was a collection of silver and charcoal gray with a countertop and island made of some glittery but hard surface.

"It's recycled glass," he said, as I ran a hand over it.

"Really?"

"Yeah, it's old bottles crushed and made smooth. That's part of the reason I chose this place. When they renovated it, they tried to make it as eco-friendly as possible."

"I didn't know you cared about the environment," I told him, impressed at this unexpected nugget.

He shrugged. "Nana again. She didn't believe in waste, and her parents were a product of the depression. She reused everything and taught me to do the same."

Once we left the kitchen, I noticed that exposed beams and brick work pervaded each room. His tan sectional stretched across his living area, and a maple wood table graced the smaller dining room.

"The table and chairs in there came with the place," he told me. "I never actually eat in there."

"Where do you eat then?"

"On the sectional mostly. Each end has a recliner."

"Do you use TV trays like Ash and I do?"

"Naw. I just do my best not to spill anything." He scratched the back of his neck. "Which doesn't always work, admittedly. Good thing I had the fabric treated to be stain resistant."

"You are such a dude," I said, pointing a finger at his chest. He took my finger and kissed it, smirking in that flirty way he had sometimes.

"You know it."

He then drew his lips along the palm of my hand, and I felt their warm softness all the way up my arm. And elsewhere. I was tingling in some interesting locations when he tugged me toward a wall covered in blinds.

"Saved one of my favorite features of this place for last." He hit a remote control I never saw him pick up, and I heard a whirring noise as the blinds were whisked away into either side of the adjoining walls.

With the blinds out of the way, I could see the glass of his floor-to-ceiling windows that made up the entirety of his exterior wall. Beyond that was Manhattan, in all its nighttime glory. I gasped. I couldn't help it. I was a New Yorker, born and bred, but the modest abodes I'd lived in had never been privy to views like this.

The skyline sparkled against the black sky while the massive rectangle of Central Park lay before me. Beyond were the myriad of bridges crossing the waters of the Hudson, a low half-moon reflecting in the water.

"My God, Trevor. This is …" I didn't know how to finish that sentence. None of my words seemed good enough to describe it.

"I like it," was all he said, uncharacteristically meek.

"Me, too."

Then, as if the majesty of the outside didn't hold the same level of fascination as his television, he did an about-face. "So, what sounds good? I have all the latest Marvel movies. Or if you want to go old school, I have the original Star

Wars trilogy, Indiana Jones franchise, or the Back to the Futures. Unless you want to watch sports." That last suggestion sounded saturated with hope, which I unfortunately had to dash.

"Not much of a sports aficionado, I'm afraid."

This was true, especially because my mother's boyfriend's favorite pastime had been baseball. He'd been a rabid fan, and if you dared interrupt while he was slumped in front of our television watching a game, there'd be hell to pay. He'd record games with a DVR and watch them over and over. The worst part was that he'd had one playing in the background when he'd hurt me. Up till then I hadn't cared about any sport much, one way or the other, but afterwards...

Yeah.

If I never heard or saw another baseball game again, it'd be too soon. Thinking about any of that made my throat dry up and my pulse run the hundred-meter dash, particularly when I thought of Ashley's advice to unload all that baggage on the father of my baby.

Ugh.

"So, a movie then?" The said father brought me back to the present. "Here." Trevor handed me the remote. "Pick whatever you want, okay? I'm going to get us something to drink. I have sweet tea, lemonade, and filtered water."

"What? No beer?" I joked past my desert-like mouth, but it might've been a little forced.

He paused beneath the arched doorway leading from his living room to his kitchen. "No, I have plenty of beer, I just didn't want to rub your nose in it." He didn't move from his spot, waiting for my answer.

"Um, anything, I guess. Is that sweet tea of yours hot or cold?"

"Cold. It's iced tea."

"Never cared much for iced tea. It's kind of bitter." I hit a button on the remote and brought up a whole slew of war movies. That would be a hell no.

"You've never had sweet tea?"

"Don't think so. I'm fine with water, though."

He disappeared and reappeared with three tall glasses. "Under no circumstances is it okay that you've come this far in life without having sweet tea. Try it. If you hate it …" The expression on his face told me he considered such a thing pure sacrilege. "Then, I brought water, too."

To placate him, I took a sip of his cherished sweet tea. And sweet was right. It burst over my taste buds like soda but without the fizz. It wasn't syrupy or saccharin-like, though. It felt fabulous on my parched throat. I took more of a gulp the next time. The more I drank, the better it tasted.

Sweet tea. Who knew?

He smiled at my newfound love of a beverage that he'd just highly recommended, then marched off to get what turned out to be a ceramic bowl full of popcorn. The buttery aroma pervaded his apartment, and he flipped on a gas fireplace, the violet and orange flames instantly coming to life.

He sat beside me then said, "Alexa, dim the lights." And his AI home system complied. This apartment was such a different beast from what I was used to. Trevor had every convenience and novel technology at his disposal. But somehow between his solid warmth at my side, the popcorn situated in his lap, and the low quavering light of both his big screen and the fireplace, I felt comfortable here. Almost at home.

I'd finally chosen the most recent Marvel movie—one I hadn't had the chance to watch either in the theater or out of it—and as it progressed, I found Trevor touching me more and more. First, the bowl went missing. Next, his arm went around my shoulders. Then, his lips brushed my temple, my hair, and the top of my ear. And almost before I was cognizant of it, I was pressing my own lips up against his.

It started out slow. One kiss. Two kisses. The movie was interesting, but the poor thing didn't hold a candle to him. Within moments our lip-locks went from leisurely to something less contained. My hands wandered from my sides to span across his broad chest, then to outline the defined musculature of his upper arms. And all the while, his lips went from kissing my neck to suckling a singular location under my ear that made me groan.

We were making out there on his fancy sectional like a pair of teenagers, and I was loving it. Losing myself in it. My fingers went up and into his hair, my nails barely scraping along his scalp, and now he was the one groaning, so I ran my nails over his scalp over and over again.

Our bodies hadn't been this close since the night we'd conceived our baby, and even then, I hadn't had my hands free. I hadn't been able to explore him at all, and while we'd both been stark naked, the blindfold meant that I hadn't seen any of his bare body before he left the hotel room.

What a travesty.

I shifted so that I could shift his Henley up and off of him, delighted to find no undershirt beneath. At last, I could feast my eyes on the glory that was Trevor Keller. There were acres of beauty before me. The broad chest that I'd studied so many times through his clothes was firm and defined, his pecs topping a torso ridged with strength.

His six-pack was drool worthy, and a line of fine hair pointed like an arrow down below his navel, vanishing under the denim of his dark jeans. Rubbing my hands across that chest and those abs did delightful things to me. I became surrounded by a fog of my own desire, and everything else in my world went fuzzy around the edges.

On a scale of one to ten, with one being asleep and ten being wildly aroused, I was at least an eleven.

While I'd been focused on him, he'd been focused on me. He'd pulled down the uppermost portion of my dress and bra without me even being aware of it, and now my breasts, swollen in preparation for our child, were exposed to his view.

"Jesus Christ, they're even darker than before, and so much like, *jigglier*."

I froze like a statue. I didn't know if it was the pregnancy hormones or what, but the areolas of my breasts had changed color from a brownish pink to much deeper chestnut shade. It meant I had to pay more attention to some of my lighter garments. Once, I'd put on a sheer bra with a white shirt with nearly disastrous results. I'd been on my way out the door when my roomie kindly pointed this out to me. Needless to say, I'd never worn that combination since.

"And … And you're all right with that?"

"Are you kidding? It's so fucking *hot*." His breathing was jagged as he cupped both his hands over my nipples then, rolling them between his finger and thumb. I gasped, the bite of pain a wakeup call after feeling so high on pleasure. "What's wrong?"

"They're sore," I confessed, already sorry. I wanted his touch so badly I almost whimpered.

But Trevor was undeterred. "How about this?" He leaned down and flicked the tip of his tongue against my nipple instead. He did it softly and with extra care, the wet warmth of his mouth around my breast as he exhaled.

"God!"

"Okay?" he asked, his speech muffled by the part of me that was inside him.

"*Yes*. So much yes."

When he gave my other nipple the same treatment, I was nearly catapulted through the roof. He used just the right amount of pressure. Enough that I felt him, without his caress causing me even the slightest amount of tenderness or discomfort.

I hadn't felt this good in so long.

His tongue licked a trail down my cleavage as I left open-mouthed kisses on his forehead. His body was against mine on the sectional. He'd pulled my legs up beside him so we could both lay lengthwise against each other. I could feel his arousal poking into my thigh as his mouth continued to worship my breasts, and I didn't want it to end or even to slow down. But then something happened that brought us both to a screeching halt.

Our son moved. And not just a little, either. The sensation was more distinct. It was as if he was performing a series of kicks or maybe even cartwheels. Trevor's chest had been against my distended tummy, so from his reaction I could tell he must've felt that *bop, bop, bop*, too.

"Whoa," he said, extricating himself from me as if I'd turned into a ticking timebomb in the past second.

"The baby's being active," I observed, hoping to diffuse whatever was making Trevor back away.

"But what does that mean? Am I hurting him? If we continue this, will it be bad for him at all?"

Thankfully, that was a question I already knew the answer to. I'd been reading about all sorts of issues and that had been one. "It's like um ... rocking the baby. And any endorphins that might be released will affect both him and me in a positive way. It wouldn't be harmful."

Then, a silent mantra played on repeat through my mind:

Please don't stop. Please don't stop. Please don't stop.

Even though he had.

He seemed to ponder what I'd said for a moment, then in an action that seemed astoundingly effortless considering my increase in mass, he lifted me into his arms.

"Good to know."

Trevor offered me his sexiest and most wolfish of grins, smashing his lips against mine with renewed gusto as he headed with absolute confidence toward what I prayed was his bedroom.

18

TREVOR

The only thing around me was Jessica. Her hair, her face, her breasts, her legs, her rounded abdomen. And everything about her was wondrous. Indescribably intoxicating.

So ungodly sexy.

Yet, the type of sexiness she exuded had altered. Not that she wasn't a feast for the eyes. It was more that her sexiness went beyond the surface level beauty that was visible by sight and touch. This woman was strong, intelligent, and working toward her dreams. As soon as she'd discovered she was carrying my son, she'd invited me to be a part of this miracle when she could've chosen to never speak to me again.

And there was something between us. Something more than our son, even. A link had been forged between us early on, and though I'd attempted to ignore it, I couldn't anymore. Especially not with her in my arms. I wanted her. Not just in my bed, but in my life. And I wanted her not only as a mother for our child, but as a lover and a friend. As a girlfriend and maybe if she agreed, even more. I wanted to take away all her worries. I wanted to give her anything and everything.

I wanted her to be mine in every single sense of the word.

Things had gotten a bit carried away in the living room, so I was glad of our son's inadvertent interruption. It gave me a chance to get my act together. To fuel my passion for her with more than brainless lust.

I'd stripped her of her bra, and now that I had her laid out across my blankets of my bed, I peeled her dress the rest of the way down, leaving a trail of kisses on each inch I'd exposed. It was torturous work because every stroke and sigh nearly robbed me of my control.

Totally worth it.

Once she was naked before me, I divested myself of the remainder of my clothing and snuggled up beside her. I needed her to know this would be more than sex to me. I was in this because I loved both the baby *and* her.

I was in love with her.

I wanted her next to me. I wanted to come home to her and see her holding our son. I wanted her and I to raise him together. To teach him how to say Mama and Daddy. To teach him how to ride a bike and root for the Saints.

I wanted it all.

I was so relieved that I'd taken a minute to light the fireplaces, both in the living room and here in the bedroom, because the firelight made her luscious copper skin radiant. It played over every one of her curves and subtle angles.

I soothed my hands and lips over every inch of her I could reach. Once I had her moaning even more distractingly than she had been on the sectional, I positioned my mouth over her core, lapping up her essence until with a cry that morphed into a long shuddering keen, she came.

And though she wasn't bound in any way, I delighted in it, in her coming all over my face. She was free to move and she had, holding on to my hair by the roots as if to ground herself. Though I'd initiated this, she'd willingly reciprocated. I found it delicious that everything she did and every response she made was of her own accord. It hadn't been a turn off at all.

Go figure.

Then, ready to burst and literally leaking for her, I placed my body over hers so I could slip inside, but it didn't quite work. I flipped us so she was on top, but she crossed her arms over herself as if uncomfortable.

"Don't like it up there?" I asked her while attempting to make my brain deal with whatever was holding us back. This proved difficult with my erection throbbing against her flawless backside.

"I don't know. I've never had sex like this before."

"Really?" I asked her, surprised. I didn't have much experience with this either since I always craved to be the one in charge.

"It's ... I feel exposed."

Enough said. I pulled her down beside me, her back to my front as I spooned her from behind. This way, I didn't feel like I might be squashing our son and she seemed more at peace with our position, as well. It took a few different tries at rearranging our hips and legs. But eventually, I found a combination that allowed me to both reach around and touch her where I wanted while still lining up so we could join our bodies together.

I stroked her drenched folds, a surge of pride blasting through me because I was the reason they were drenched in the first place. Maybe it was tacky, thinking of her with my inner caveman like that, but I couldn't help it. Unlike any of my other sexual partners, I felt territorial when it came to Jessica. The love and passion I felt for her made facilitating and claiming each one of her climaxes an absolute mandate.

Though it might be best for me to keep that to myself.

After I made her come again with my fingers—feeling her let go like this was officially my highest achievement—I ever so carefully slid into place inside her. Once I was fully seated, my hips flush to her ass, I wrapped my arms around her shoulders. Gently twisting her face around so I could kiss those juicy lips of her again, I held her from behind, my tongue plunging into her mouth the same way my erection had buried itself in her core.

I'd never held a woman like this, not during sex or at any other time, but the feeling of it transcended every sensation I'd ever felt. Then, I understood why. This was what happened when two people make love instead of fucking. It was new and magnificent and the best thing ever. We undulated together, our pace accelerating at the same time. We were building something in concert, in sync, and when I felt her start to tighten around me, she called out.

"Trevor, oh God, yes, *Trevor!*"

And I was a goner. Her orgasm inevitably triggered mine and as it swept over me, I held her firmly, needing to be as close to her as possible. Some sort of peculiar heat burned behind my eyes, and as soon as I recognized it, I screwed my eyelids shut against the onslaught. I was honestly a little freaked out. Sex had never made me emotional before.

Luckily, after a tenuous moment where I was afraid I might embarrass myself, it passed.

Holy shit.

Bobbing around the lands of unmitigated bliss, we laid there together as our heart rates dropped back into the normal range. We stayed physically connected as the minutes passed, and I assumed she'd drifted off to sleep when she spoke.

"I *so* needed that."

"Me, too," I admitted.

"Ever since I've been pregnant, I've been really..."

"Horny?" I supplied, more than familiar with the concept. She chuckled, and I felt her clench down on me when she did. Not that I minded. My shaft might be softening, but I could be up and running in a minute or two should she need my services again.

I almost felt like standing too and providing her with a salute.

"Yeah. Ready to combust at a moment's notice."

"Welcome to my world, baby. I've been like that since I turned twelve."

"Are all men like that?" she asked, sounding genuinely curious.

"I think so. It's a wonder we get anything nonsexual accomplished at all, when I think about it."

I love you, I almost added. It was right there. Instead, I hugged her and asked, "Do you believe in heaven?"

Where the hell had *that* come from?

"Like clouds and angels and pearly gates?"

"Yeah."

"I don't know. Maybe. How about you?"

"Definitely. I want to think that when our son bursts on the scene that Nana's spirit with be here, wooden spoon in hand and stirring a pot as she smiles at him."

My eyes went hot again. What the actual fuck was the matter with me? I hadn't been this upset even when Nana died. At least not outwardly. Why was I losing my grip all of a sudden? It was disturbing. Time to concentrate on something else.

"You never talk about your parents or grandparents. Are they still alive?" I asked her. I'd always avoided digging too deeply, but things between us had shifted, and now felt like as good a time as ever to inquire about this.

"My maternal grandparents aren't," she said, after a lengthy pause. "I'm not sure about my parents, or the grandparents, on the other side."

"Why not?"

"I never knew my father or his side of the family."

"Oh," I said, treading cautiously. This felt like a touchy subject. "What about your mom? Did you two have a falling out or something?"

"You could say that."

"That sucks. I'm sorry." I wondered if this lack of support from her family was why she seemed to struggle so much financially.

She'd gone somewhat stiff in my arms when she'd mentioned her mother, and I waited for her to relax again. She didn't, though. If anything, the stiffness of her posture only seemed to become worse. I heard her take a breath and then, another. I was just about to ask her about it when she spoke.

"I have something I need to tell you."

There was a tone in Jessica's voice, the kind you might hear in a little kid's when they're terrified. It knocked me out of my hesitation. It was past time that she knew.

"You can tell me anything, Jessica. I love you."

This was followed by several unspooled seconds of ringing silence.

"You remember when I told you about my miscarriage?" she sputtered out, at length.

Wow, that wasn't the reaction I'd expected.

"Yeah."

"That pregnancy was what caused the falling out between me and my mother. When she found out, she kicked me out."

"Christ, seriously?" I exclaimed, horrified. "Didn't you say you were only seventeen when that happened?"

"Yeah," she whispered.

"Then, your mother was a fucking bitch," I spat out, enraged on her behalf. Teen pregnancies happened sometimes. And such a thing was no reason to force a girl out of her own home. Even anything, she would've needed that home more than ever. I wanted to smash something, but Jessica needed me to comfort her. "That is unforgivable."

"There's more, though." Her whisper grew tremulous and even less audible. "I didn't get pregnant by some boy at school. The fath––It was my mother's boyfriend. He …" She didn't go on, and I tried to be patient. An ominous feeling settled over my skin as lead the size of a cannonball dropped into my stomach. "He raped me."

And though my vision went red with rage, I continued to lay there as if what she'd just said was okay. It wasn't. It *so* wasn't. But I couldn't lose my shit in front of her, so I made myself stay prone at her side.

"Sh-she evicted me, and I was so afraid and m-miserable." Jessica was sobbing now. "I spent that night outside in the c-cold, then went to stay at my friends' houses for a while. I miscarried before I r-reached my second trimester. I know I sh-should've told you all this before, and I'm s-sorry." One distant corner of my brain warned me that she shouldn't be the one apologizing, but I couldn't seem to make myself speak.

I knew I should be doing something other than laying there like a bump on a log, but my ability to take the proper action had become compromised. I was no longer touching her, and if I allowed myself to move even a little, I would be like a grenade without its pin, guaranteed to explode. So I went on laying there feeling useless, yet remaining hopelessly mute.

Say something, the one tiny piece of my consciousness told me. *Make her feel better.*

But my mouth refused to work.

She didn't turn towards me. Instead, she wiggled herself until she managed to push off the mattress. I didn't help her because it took everything I had to restrain my violent feelings toward the bastard who'd injured her.

The room was dim, lit only by my fireplace, but I cinched my eyes shut anyway, listening as she struggled back into her dress. I sensed when she left my bedroom. And then I listened as she moved through my apartment. I heard the sound of my front door clicking shut. She didn't slam it like I expected her to.

Then, there was nothing but quiet.

Again, the part of my brain that had been capable of making rational decisions screamed at me to get up and go after her, to show her I gave a damn before it was too late. But I didn't. Instead, I sat up, and just like I'd feared, this movement caused a chain reaction within me. I full out sprinted into my gym and smacked my fist into the large punching bag there, roaring with fury as I did.

I couldn't have said what spilled from my mouth. Obscenities and curses, mostly. Bellows of rage. I knew I'd called Jessica's mother and boyfriend every filthy word in the English language. Still naked as the day I was born, I beat that bag until I knew it wasn't going to be enough, then set my sights on the brick of my apartment wall.

It was only after that, when I was flat out on my face with blood pouring from my ruined knuckles and my right hand screaming in agony that any rational thought returned. I'd always had a dark side to myself that I kept hidden. I let it out a little at a time with bondage sex and an hour or two in my gym. But this time, that darkness had taken me over. It'd made me freeze at the worst possible time.

And I knew with great certainty that I'd well and truly fucked everything up with the love of my life.

19

JESSIE

MAY

*M*istakes. I was so goddamn sick of making them. I'd made the mistake of agreeing to take the job the Wish Maker had offered me. I'd made the mistake of going on that date with Trevor. And now, I'd made the mistake of telling him the truth about my past. I never should have. I'd felt used up and ruined ever since that horrendous night when I was seventeen, and now, Trevor saw me for what I was. Damaged goods.

Good going, Jess.

For a week, there was no contact of any kind between Trevor and me. None. Then one week turned into two and two into three. When my next doctor's appointment arrived, I went by myself, wondering if he'd show up separately.

He didn't.

After that, my appointments would increase to bi-weekly in preparation for birth. I texted him a copy of these dates and waited to see if I'd receive any sort of response. I did. But it was unsatisfying.

Thanks, it read. *I'll do my best to attend.*

That's all it said. I psychoanalyzed the hell out of his words, even sharing them to Ashley to get her opinion. Why did he sound so formal? Did he really appreciate me sending him the information or not? Would he be there to face the gulf of awkwardness that now lay between us like the Grand Canyon?

The only answer I would receive was to that last question because the appointment came and went without him.

So sorry, but I can't be there today. Work is insane right now. Raincheck for the next one? His text said.

But he didn't come to that one, either. Nor did he come to the next. Clearly, whatever I thought might've been burgeoning between us had ceased to exist. He'd told me he loved me, but we'd been naked at the time. I should've known such a promise was destined to be broken. If he'd truly loved me, he wouldn't have abandoned me—abandoned *us*. I felt like a moron for hoping. When would I learn my lesson? First my mother and now him.

Maybe I was simply impossible to love.

The next month passed in a whirl of Zumba classes, fitness training sessions, and doctor's appointments. Trevor had continued to text me apologies for his absence, even when I ceased all communication with him, but I no longer cared. I knew when to cut my losses. I'd done it before, after all.

Even if doing it this time made my injured heart bleed harder than ever.

Leading my Zumba class had become more and more difficult physically, and I finally went to Lance to request that he find another instructor to fill in for me. He'd taken one long look at me and agreed, even offering me a couple of new fitness training clients to help pad out my income. I appreciated it.

So that morning in May as flower petals blew in the wind like confetti, I was on my way to the CrossFit gym to put one of these clients through his paces. The guy had a bit of a paunch and said he wanted to get into shape. As a corporate executive, he spent more time behind a desk than anywhere else, and since he'd been divorced for a few years, he decided he needed that to change.

I was happy to guide him, even though the mention of his corporate job reminded me of Trevor. But then again, most things did. Anyone in a suit. Anyone with light eyes. Any guy with a beard, a goatee, or scruff on their chins. The smell of pizza. Seeing a pineapple. Every blue SUV. The list went on and on.

"Fifteen," I counted out, as my client gasped through a set of jump squats. "Sixteen. Come on, four more. Seventeen. Eighteen. Nine—"

I broke off, suddenly feeling strange. Something seemed to be going wrong inside my skull, and my vision dimmed. I took one step backwards as blackness descended over me like a curtain.

Before I could do or say anything else, there was a sensation of plummeting to the ground.

And then, there was nothing at all.

~

I woke on the floor of the gym feeling as if I'd been slammed into by a Mack truck. Every single muscle in my body was sore, and I couldn't make heads or tails out of anything. It took me a while to figure out why I was laying down and even who it was surrounding me. People's faces hovered above me with expressions of exaggerated distress, but I didn't know why.

All I wanted to do was lay here. Why weren't people leaving me alone so I could rest?

Ultimately, the thoughts that had refused to coalesce started to rearrange themselves until I recognized a few of the people overhead.

"Ash … Lance … Chuck …" Chuck was my fitness client. There were other people there, too, people in dark uniform shirts with medical insignia on their chests, but I didn't know them. "Why are you here?"

I attempted to sit up. It occurred to me that being sprawled on the floor like this might be bad for the baby. The second I moved, though, the room swirled violently.

"Hold still," two people commanded me at once. One was one of the medical people and one was Ashley. It was the uniformed person who spoke again. "We need you to stay where you are, Jessie."

How do you know my name? The question blinked through my consciousness, but it wasn't what I said aloud.

"What's wrong?" I asked instead, but no one answered me. My best friend stared at me like I was on death's front door. Lance's eyes were enormous in his face. And Chuck was busy giving an account of something to another medical person.

"She went down like a ton of bricks. I barely caught her in time. Then, she started shaking real hard and flinging her arms and legs all over the place. I didn't know what to do, so I held on to her." Chuck had a shiner coming up on his left eye. Where had that come from? And who was he talking about going down like a ton of bricks and shaking?

"Calling nine-one-one was the right thing to do, sir. Do you need something for your eye?"

He waved it off. "I'm fine. I just want to make sure Jessie is okay."

"What's wrong?" I asked again, louder this time. "What's happening?"

"You collapsed, Jess," Ashley said, her complexion white as a sheet. "Chuck saw you have a seizure."

"A seizure?" I couldn't make those words compute. Didn't seizures only happen to people who were epileptic or something? I'd never been diagnosed with that sort of disorder. Had I? I reached up and held my head, but even raising my arms that much hurt. The room continued to swim, too. I really wished the world would stop buzzing and jackknifing around like this.

And then, the blackness took over again.

∽

Waking took time and effort to accomplish this time around. It was far more laborious than I could ever remember it being prior to this. It was like those dreams where you're racing down a hallway towards an open door but can't ever seem to reach your destination. It was horrifying, and yet my sluggish brain kept me from panicking.

I was too tired and sore to panic.

Little by little, though, I found my way back to reality. And it wasn't a reality I liked. I was in a white room that beeped erratically, smelled like rubbing alcohol, and was far brighter than I thought it needed to be. I felt pressure on my belly and glanced down at a sensor strapped low on my round abdomen.

I bolted up, or tried to. What I probably actually did was spasm upwards by an inch or two only to slump right back down onto my mattress. The mattress of this narrow bed. A hospital bed.

Oh, God.

"Is the baby okay?" my question came out half-garbled as if my mouth wouldn't work correctly. What the hell was wrong with me? Had I had a stroke?

"Yes, Jess. Relax," Ashley said from behind me. She materialized from somewhere slightly to the left of me. "They think everything is going to be all right."

"Tell me," I said, but my words came out as less of an order and more of a plea.

"You have a condition they called Eclampsia. It's basically a severe form of pre-eclampsia or high blood pressure that causes seizures in pregnant women. They've got you on a whole cocktail of medication that will hopefully help."

"How long have I been here?"

"A few hours. They ran all these tests and things while you were out. They're doing their best to make sure you don't have any more seizures. How are you feeling?"

"Kind of rough," I said, honestly. Though rough was an understatement. I was still struggling to wrangle my thoughts into anything decipherable. Also, even though I knew I should be more alert and finding out more answers, I could barely keep my eyes open.

"Rest, then, honey," my best friend said, brushing my hair back from my forehead.

And since I felt more exhausted than I ever had in my life, I did.

20

TREVOR

"What do you have for me, Hendricks?" I half yelled into my work landline, gripping the receiver so hard I heard a little crack as I rushed to my feet. The action caused my hand to twinge due to the three bones within it that had so recently been broken, but physical pain didn't matter to me. All I did was switch the phone to my left less injured hand.

"Nine six three dash two three five." Hendricks cigar-stained voice rattled back. "It's his inmate number. He's currently incarcerated at Lincoln Correctional Facility. Serving twenty to life for first degree murder."

My knees went weak as my ass hit my office chair. Well, it wasn't my own chair since I was working out of an office in Dallas rather than back at the city. Fucking finally. *Finally*, I had the information I'd been seeking. And, better yet, it was good news. The best. I had this insane impulse to laugh maniacally like the Joker. Nothing about this situation was funny, but my sanity had long since left the building.

I'd felt half deranged from the moment Jessica had told me about the hideous events of her past. Of the suffering she'd endured. An odd switch had been flipped inside me when she'd explained that her mother's boyfriend had raped her. That his unforgivable act had impregnated her. That her mother had blamed Jessica instead of her goddamn rapist and thrown her own seventeen-year-old daughter out to the curb like trash.

I hadn't reacted when she spilled her heart out to me. I hadn't moved a muscle for fear that I would do some crazed thing that might freak her out. I'd waited for her to leave, even knowing deep down that she needed more from me. Once she was gone, I'd beaten the fuck out of my punching bag, then hauled off and thrown my fist into the decades old brick wall.

And then, I did it again.

Hence, the broken hand.

That jolt of pain had almost equaled me out and balanced me, but not quite. I'd lost any balance or equilibrium I might've ever had, and it wasn't back even now. Hell, it might never be back. Nothing had felt right since except for latching onto a single life's purpose.

Track that motherfucker down.

Those words are the only things that had kept me from winding up in a padded cell under lock and key. That thought had galvanized me, mobilized me into an action that did good rather than harm. I had to find this evil son of a bitch and make certain he could never hurt Jessica ever again.

Ironic that motherfucker was actually an accurate description in this case.

This errant thought was not unlike others I'd been experiencing. It was unsettling, this feeling of being so out of control. I'd wondered more than once if I'd had some sort of mental break, if I had legitimately become certifiable over all this. But then, I'd pushed any concerns about that back. My stability or lack thereof wasn't as important as what I was doing now.

I knew his name, though he'd apparently held multiple identities over the years. The slippery asshole had been born Brighton Jennings Caulfield the Third. He sounded like old money, but he wasn't. His grandfather had been successful, but his dad had run the family business straight into the ground. Mister "the third" had been worthless from the get-go.

He'd been a mean kid in juvie. In his twenties, he'd committed a series of misdemeanors like shoplifting and petty larceny. He'd been accused of more heinous acts, but there hadn't been enough evidence to convict the bastard. Then, in his thirties, he'd upped his game by getting involved in organized crime. Around the same time, he'd also gotten involved with Jessica's mother.

"Send hard copies to my address," I told Hendricks, the private investigator I'd hired through the Wish Maker the day after I'd pounded my fist. "Maintain tabs on him." Without another word, I hung up. I abandoned the company's landline and retrieved my cell.

"I have a target I need destroyed," I said, sounding relatively calm considering what I was asking.

"Such a contract would be three times the rate of your other arrangement with us," the Wish Maker replied, her ancient voice benign despite her words.

"I agree to those terms. I'm texting the info now. When will this be complete?"

After a short pause, she answered, "Seventy-two hours."

There was a click. It was done.

I peered at my phone, taking note of the date. An entire month had gone by since that night with Jessica. It seemed impossible. Time had quit behaving correctly. It'd jump past me like it was on fast-forward, then drag by as if it had stopped altogether. These four weeks had been nothing but distracted work through my bank and demanding constant updates from Hendricks. I remembered next to nothing else about this time.

I'd been reprimanded by my boss. I'd gone from a rising star in the company to a guy holding on to his job by his fingertips. It was why I was here in Dallas now putting out fires in a satellite office rather than back in Manhattan. Lars had been watching me with a gimleted eye as soon as I'd started to go off the rails.

Initially, he'd been sympathetic. He was a fair man. But over time, he'd become impatient with me. I hadn't explained any of the reasons behind the abrupt gap in my performance. So, he'd sent me here with an ultimatum to increase this office's accounts or else. Well, the "or else" had been more implied than stated as fact, but it'd been there.

I'd disappointed him, and once upon a time, I would have been upset by this. The opportunity he'd granted me had been why I relocated in the first place. My whole adult life had been about my career. But now, it wasn't. It was about retribution. It was about making sure Jessica was safe, and would always be safe.

Even though I knew she must hate me now.

I deserved her hatred. So many times I'd wanted to go to her, to talk to her and apologize. I wanted to hold her in my arms and assure her that everything would be all right. But I hadn't been able to do that. I couldn't. Not until I knew for a fact it would be the truth.

And the only way to do that was end the man who'd hurt her.

I'd already performed a few of my nana's old rituals. Not the old Hollywood use of Voodoo dolls being stuck by needles, but chants asking the spirit world to expose this evil man to the light. To unearth him like a skeleton being expelled from the proverbial closet.

Now, he had been, and the wheels were in motion to take him out for good.

I'd expected to feel better having taken this step. Relieved somehow. But maybe that would only come when I knew him to be dead. Then, at that point, maybe I could go back to living my life again. What was left of it.

A peal of thunder made me peer out the window into a stormy sky. It was mid-afternoon, but the sky had grown as dark as night. A whipping thunderstorm had arrived without warning—the last glimpse I'd taken outside had been of a sunny Texas day. I'd forgotten how different the weather was here, how much more tumultuous. It reminded me of myself.

This office faced east toward Louisiana, towards home. I was closer to New Orleans than I'd been in months, yet it still felt as far away as another planet. I'd considered talking to my best bud more than once about my current situation, but I hadn't done it.

Jax was happy in his life. He was settled and at peace for the first time in years. Bugging him with my current state of insanity seemed unfair somehow, inappropriate. So I hadn't done it, but for some reason, now that I'd just ordered a real-life hit on another human being, I felt more tempted to reach out to him than I had in a long time.

Maybe because I felt like a blissful family life—even though it'd nearly been within my grasp—wasn't in the cards for me.

I'd allowed my obsession with Jessica's rapist to consume me rather than spending time with her. But I just couldn't face her without a gift in hand, and the best gift I could offer her was the knowledge that that man could never touch her again.

I still held my cell loosely in my hand when it buzzed with an incoming call. I glanced at the screen, wondering if I'd managed to summon a call from Jax out of the ether, but I hadn't. The call was from Jessica.

I hesitated as the icy fingers of foreboding itched up my spine. Other than texts, I hadn't communicated with her at all. Even though keeping my distance from her until I'd resolved the situation fully was necessary, it also sucked. I missed her morning, noon, and night. But talking to her might wear away at my resolve to finish what I'd started, so I let the call go to voicemail.

There was a second call and voicemail, followed by a text. The intensity of the foreboding I felt increased by a factor of ten, and I gave in to my curiosity and read the text.

Emergency. This is Ashley. Jess collapsed and has had two seizures so far. She's being taken to Mount Sinai Hospital.

~

"She said you can't come in."

Jessica's roommate's rejection at the door of her hospital room sent me into a tailspin of frustration. I'd immediately gone to the airport to try to catch a flight, but the storm had delayed or cancelled most of the flights. Once it passed, there were no seats on the flights available, so I had to go on standby and wait.

By the time a seat opened up at last, I'd been at that damn airport for eight hours. It was the next morning, and I still hadn't departed from Dallas. Then, there'd been another issue at La Guardia, and they'd rerouted us to Newark. The drive had been bumper to bumper, and I'd nearly bellowed at my taxi driver, incensed.

The end result was that I hadn't been able to get back to New York for a day and a half.

"You're the one who contacted me, Ashley," I reminded her, thrusting my hands behind my back to hide the fact that I was clenching them hard enough to turn them white. "At least tell me if she's okay. If the baby's okay..."

"They're under observation," she said angrily, then lowered her voice. "I reached out to you because she's been trying to talk to you for ages. But as soon as I told her you were here, she said she didn't want to see you."

"I flew all the way from Dallas," I said, working this from an angle of entreaty. "That's why I was late getting here."

"You're a *month* late, Trevor," came Jessica's alto voice beyond Ashley, and my heart caught. I hadn't heard that voice in far too long. "You don't get to blame this on some business trip."

"Jessica, I—"

"Go," she cut me off. "You're not welcome here."

Not welcome.

Something went wrong inside my chest. It was as if her words had hacked into me like a serrated blade. I'd known she might feel like this but hearing it with my own ears awakened something in me that had been shut down for weeks. I loved this woman. I ached for this woman.

"Jessica, please …"

"Sir." A deep voice issued from behind me. I turned to see an African American man of about my height but with a good fifty pounds on me staring me down. On his lapel was a badge that said 'Security.' "I'm going to have to ask you to vacate this facility."

I opened my mouth to explain that I loved her and that she's carrying my baby, but then I realized that none of that mattered. All the decisions I'd been making were from wanting to do the right thing, but in that moment, I took the time to look at things from Jessica's point of view.

She didn't know what I'd been doing or why because I hadn't told her. All she knew was that she'd shared this deep dark secret with me, and I'd frozen up solid. I hadn't come to visit her. I missed all her doctor's appointments. From her perspective, she wouldn't see my behavior as anything but leaving her on her own.

Jesus Christ. What kind of asshole *was* I?

The security guy was standing toe to toe with me, his expression one of quiet menace, and I knew any further arguments I might make would only go against me. So, I pivoted and trudged my way toward the exit.

I wandered around the outside perimeter of the hospital for the rest of the night, not wanting to leave despite knowing I wouldn't be allowed back in. Other than finding out that the mother of my child had experienced two seizures and was being observed, I didn't know much. She'd been well enough to tell me to get out, so I guessed that was something.

But I didn't know why she'd had the seizures to start with. I'd Googled seizures already and what I'd found hadn't exactly made me feel better. It was such a dangerous condition. People fucking *died* from seizures sometimes.

I imagined Jessica thrashing around and then dying before anyone could save her or our child, and I dropped right where was I was, my knees hitting the pavement hard enough to scrape them raw. I hardly registered this, though. My mind filled with images of losing her and the baby, each one worse than the last, and I buried my face in my hands against the onslaught.

I didn't know how long I remained there.

It began to rain on me, but I didn't move. The sun came up and the rain ceased, but I didn't move. My ass went numb, but I didn't move. It wasn't until a rotund lady with ebony skin and long braids came by in scrubs that I even looked up.

"Hon, are you all right?"

I was nowhere near the vicinity of all right, but I nodded.

"Okay, but a man in an Armani suit and expensive shoes, sitting on the ground between the parking garage and the entrance isn't the most routine thing I've ever encountered. Are you sick?"

I shook my head.

"Injured?"

I shook it again.

"Drunk?"

This time, I spoke. "I wish."

"Then, why're you here, sweet-cheeks?"

"Came to visit someone. She doesn't want to see me."

She cast me a knowing look. "This someone your girl?"

"She was."

With a groan, she sat beside me, her fragrance reminding me of something. Baby powder. Maybe it shouldn't have inspired my trust in her, but it did.

"Let me tell you a little bit about us women. Forget all that chocolate and flowers nonsense, though those are nice, too. The main thing any woman wants from a man in a relationship is love and trust."

"What if I already ruined that?"

"Did you ruin the love part or the trust part or both?"

I sighed, my throat clogged with something I didn't want to look at too closely. "Both."

"Then you need to do one thing with everything you've got."

"What's that?"

"Fight for her."

21

JESSIE

All the way home in the cab I'd been dreading ascending those three flights of stairs up into our apartment. I was so glad to be out of the hospital, but Dr. Carrey and the physicians on duty at Mount Sinai had all monitored my condition and agreed.

Bedrest.

I'd be on twenty-four-hour bedrest for one entire month. Even though I felt tired, I couldn't imagine staying down that long. I was an active girl with too much to do, and I'd told my doctors that. I'd argued my side. They'd listened and then Dr. Carrey had said the thing that had halted my debate in its tracks.

"If you refuse to rest, you could lose this baby."

I couldn't argue with that.

Other than getting up to use the bathroom and doctor's appointments, I was to stay off my feet and away from stress. I was also on a couple of different medications to keep my blood pressure in check. Rather than the bi-weekly appointments I'd originally had, I now had weekly visits on my agenda.

Something to look forward to.

Yay. End sarcasm.

Ashley was beside me in our taxi, picking at her cuticles again. She did this when nervous or bored, so I wasn't sure which emotion was getting the better of her. My son and I were out of the hospital, which meant we were out of the proverbial woods. Then, as the cab crossed onto our street, she glanced up and narrowed her eyes at something. I followed her gaze.

Not something. But some*one*.

Trevor.

He sat there on the outside of our building, looking worse than I'd ever seen him. For about sixty seconds, my heart went out to him. The phrase, "what the cat dragged in" came to mind. He appeared, well … bedraggled. The more I studied his appearance, the more I noticed. He was wearing his usual fancy suit, but it looked like he'd slept in it. His dress shoes were dirty and possibly wet, and skin shone out at his knee—his pant leg been torn, too.

Only after Jessica helped me out of the cab did he lift his head, and then, I couldn't help but say something.

"Were you mugged?"

His face looked like raw hamburger, red and swollen. His eyes were puffy and bloodshot. Like he'd been smacked around or was hungover. Or, like maybe he'd been crying. But then I forced myself to cut off any sympathy for him. So what if he'd been crying. He'd sure as hell caused me plenty of tears. Turnabout was fair play, right?

I steeled myself with as much righteous indignation as I could muster.

"No. I just needed to see you, needed to apologize." He sounded awful. Like he had the world's worst head cold.

Stay pissed off, Jess.

"We've gone pretty far past apologies, Trevor," I told him, proud at the steadiness of my voice. "You had months to apologize, and you didn't."

"I should have."

Yes. "But you didn't," I repeated.

"I need to tell you something important. Something that'll affect both your life and the baby's. Will you let me say it?" he asked.

"If I let you, will you go as soon as you're through?" I volleyed back.

He gazed into my face, his amber eyes fully meeting mine for the first time since I'd told him everything. "Yes."

I allowed him to follow us up. It took longer than usual because I had to lean on Ashley so much. After getting me situated on our loveseat, my best friend remained nearby. "Need anything else?" She'd already secured me a tall glass of water and an apple.

"I'm good."

Ashley squinted at Trevor like she might a stain she couldn't scrub out. "I'm just a yell away," she told me, then disappeared into her room.

Only after she'd closed her door did he speak.

"I found him. Your mother's boyfriend. He's in prison and won't be alive much longer."

I gawked at him in disbelief. Of all the things I'd imagined him saying, it wasn't this. It took me a moment to string my words together enough to manufacture a clear thought. "Do you mean he's in some state on Death's Row?"

"I mean I hired the Wish Maker to take him out."

"Trevor," I whispered, aghast. "You can't do that. It's murder."

"I had to. I did this for you and the baby."

"I don't understand."

He began to pace, obviously agitated. "When you told me what happened to you, I lost it there for a while. The thought of him being out there where he could hurt you again was untenable to me. I couldn't allow it. So I've been hunting for him and two days ago, found him. Yesterday, I put the wheels in motion that'll make sure he'll never pose a threat to you ever again."

"You've spent the past two months searching for him?"

"Yes."

"Why didn't you tell me?"

"Because I wanted it taken care of up front. I don't want you to have to worry about him anymore," he said, as if this were something people did every day.

"That still doesn't explain why you didn't tell me. Why you ignored me all this time. You vanished, Trevor, right out of my life." I patted my big belly. "Out of *our* lives. Do you have any idea how horrible that was for me?"

He ceased his pacing and ran a hand through his hair. "Look, I know you may not accept this, but I love you. I had to protect you before I came back to you. I should've told you, but I didn't realize it'd take so long."

I shook my head at him. "Do you even hear yourself right now? You're not making a lick of sense."

"I know, okay," he sputtered out, agreeing with me but sounding argumentative just the same. "I know. I have no excuse for my behavior, except to say that I couldn't handle what you told me. Picturing that, imagining you like that, I lost my collective shit, Jessica. I snapped, and it was only after I heard your voice in the hospital sending me away that I came back to myself."

"But…"

"No, please. Let me finish. Then, it occurred to me that concentrating so hard on tracking that bastard down to the exclusion of all else was the wrong thing to do. I should've stood by you, been there for you, and I wasn't. I'm so sorry, Jessica. Beyond sorry. I know it's not enough. I know it's too little too late, but I have to say it. Leaving you all alone like I did makes me the same as your mom, and I doubt I'll ever forgive myself for that."

His eyes had filled, and his voice broke on his last sentence. He had to pause before he could go on. "I love you and our son more than anything. I want to be a part of your lives. I want us to be a family, and I hope you'll give me the chance to prove it."

For a long minute I remained quiet. It wasn't because I wanted to watch him twist forlornly in the wind, it was because I didn't know what to say. He'd burned me so badly when he'd gone off on his own like that, but I couldn't deny that being in a whole healthy family was something I'd always yearned for. Always.

But one thing stuck out to me beyond his declaration, and it had to be addressed. "Did you seriously hire someone to kill Bright?" I didn't like saying his name. I hadn't said it in years, but I needed to be crystal clear about this.

"I did."

"Has it happened yet? Is he dead?"

Trevor scratched the back of his neck. "I don't know. I think the Wish Maker will inform me when it's done."

"Can you stop it?"

"Why?"

"Because I need you to. I don't know if there'll be a chance to repair our relationship otherwise. Our son deserves better than a father who's a murderer."

His expression became stricken. Instead of saying anything, he pulled out his phone and put it to his ear. "I need to cancel a contract," he spoke rapidly. "If it hasn't already been carried out, don't go through with the hit on Brighton Jennings Caulfield the third."

He listened, and all my muscles vibrated with tension. The wait seemed to go on forever, and as if our son was responding to it, he kicked me in the bladder. I hauled myself off the loveseat to go to the bathroom. When I came back out, Trevor was there on the other side of the door.

"Did you hear anything?"

He nodded. "She cancelled the hit. It's over." He offered me his arm and I took it, letting him help me back to my seat.

We sat there together talking for quite a while after that. There was no intimate touching, no kissing or anything like that. But we both came clean about everything that had transpired during his absence.

A couple of hours later, he hugged me on his way out, telling me he'd be back the next day. And he was. Things were not as they'd once been between us, and I doubted they ever would be. But I did have hope that we might be able to reach a place where we could both find what we needed.

Only time would tell.

TREVOR

"I have some more suggestions. Drake, Drew, David, and Davenport," I said, grinning into the phone, even though Jessica couldn't see it. We'd been talking baby names for a few weeks now and we'd already cycled through the alphabet once. Now, we'd come back up to the Ds, and I perpetually threw an oddball in there just for fun.

"Davenport, huh? I kinda like that one."

My grin drained right off my face. "No way."

"Yes, way. He sounds quite dashing."

"He sounds like a douchewad."

She laughed and I relaxed at the sound of it. She was yanking my chain, thank God. "You're way too easy to mess with."

Slowly, I'd been making inroads into healing our once decimated relationship. It was different than it had been before, more of an open friendship, and I could live with that. I'd have to. Beggers couldn't be choosers.

Ever since the day I'd called off the hit on her mother's boyfriend, Jessica had been willing to talk to me. At first, I'd been a brief daily visit. I'd pop in and check on her, bringing her lunch or a special pillow to support her back, or something for the baby. Then, we added texts and calls to the mix, too. Now, we rarely went more than two hours during the day without some sort of conversation, even if it was just a joke.

I sent her a graphic from an old Far Side cartoon showing a doctor holding a bunny over a pregnant woman in the delivery room. It was captioned: An amateur magician as well as an obstetrician, the doctor felt it was important to bring some humor into the delivery room.

"How you like the cartoon I sent you?"

"I can't make up my mind on whether it's lame or funny," she said, "but that doesn't mean I want you pulling any stunts on the day in question. Whenever that's going to be."

The mother of my son was miserable. Her due date had passed ten days ago, and I knew she was having issues sleeping. I knew because she would text me at three in the morning asking me to send her more jokes. I'd taken to collecting them for this specific purpose. Sometimes, she'd laugh one minute only to burst into tears the next, but I'd learned that it usually wasn't a crisis unless it went on for longer than a minute or two. Usually.

She'd been off bed rest for the past five weeks now, and she was so disappointed that the contractions hadn't begun instantly. Dr. Carrey had given us a few options to get nature to take its course faster. So far, we'd tried going on long walks, as well as working out at her gym—low impact and gentle calisthenics only, of course. She'd tried castor oil, but it'd made her feel nauseous to smell it, so drinking the junk was a no-go.

I couldn't blame her on that one.

We'd also tried spicy foods. Pineapple, both on pizza and fresh chunks straight from the cutting board. We tried herbal teas, and I'd given her several back and neck massages, all with no success. The other options offered were more risqué, so we hadn't gone that far yet. Though I tended to give her a peck on the lips when I said goodbye, that's as sexual as we'd been with one another since that godforsaken night when I lost my fucking mind.

But I tried not to think about that too much.

She'd told me she looked like a beached whale, and though I always told her that wasn't true—she was just as gorgeous as ever—I hadn't pushed the issue. The two times we'd had sex had led to some fairly horrible dissension between us, so I wasn't going to initiate anything in that direction.

At least not anytime soon.

My body adamantly disagreed with this decision, of course. I was hard around Jessica all the time. And I mean, all the time. I'd taken to pulling my shirt out of my suit pants or jeans to disguise this. I didn't want to pressure her. I needed her and my son in my life too badly to allow my passion for her to wreck what we'd rebuilt together.

It might sound counterintuitive, but I loved her too much to do the two things we hadn't yet tried: Nipple stimulation and sexual intercourse.

Also, while I'd made it a point during all my goodbyes to say I loved her, she'd never said it back to me. I'd come to the conclusion that while we'd become friends and would soon be parents together, we might never go back to any sort of romantic relationship. Not that I believed in never saying never, but I needed to be realistic about our future. She'd expressed that she wanted me in her life and in our baby's, that she cared about me, too. But that's as far as it went.

Until later that same night.

I'd spent the evening with her because Ashley had gone out of town with her mom. She hadn't felt well that day, so I'd done my best to cheer her up by showing her silly video clips on YouTube.

"I'm so sick of being pregnant," she'd complained, rubbing her vast belly. "Come out, already!" She ordered our son, and while early on I might've bit back a grin at this, tonight I hadn't.

He kept kicking her every time she found a comfortable position, making her groan in discomfort. Around midnight, she'd drifted off on her loveseat, and I'd carried her to her bed, carefully settling her in. Even as pregnant as she was, her tiny frame didn't weigh much. And I enjoyed taking care of her like this.

On the way home, I saw an email from Lars. Luckily, I'd been able to smooth things over with my boss at work. I told him I'd had some personal issues that had impacted me in a way I'd been unprepared for. I'd even confided about the health scare of the mother of my child, and he'd been forgiving enough to give me a second shot.

Had Lars been anything other than a nice guy, I probably would've been fired outright. I appreciated his patience with me, but for the first time ever, if I had to make a choice between my career and my personal life—i.e. Jessica and my son—my personal life would win hands down. She would always be my top priority, and this time, I'd made sure she knew that.

I'd been in a sound sleep when her ringtone went off on my phone. I jolted up in my bed, reaching blindly for that rectangle of light. "Jessica?" I mumbled, still half out of it.

"Trevor? I need you!"

That woke me up. I was on my feet pushing my legs into some sweats and tennis shoes. "On my way."

I didn't remember the drive from Manhattan to Brooklyn. All I knew was she needed me there. Only as I pulled up did it occur to me that she might be in labor. Without Ashley there, she had to depend on either me, a taxi, or an ambulance to get her to the hospital. I snatched my keys from the ignition and sprinted at full speed up her three flights of stairs.

"Jessica, open up. Are you okay?" I shouted through her door, and she opened it a few seconds later. I studied her, looking for signs of pain, but while her eyes were glittering in an unusual way, I didn't see anything obviously wrong.

She was standing there in a sleeveless maternity nightgown, looking both cute and sexy, her dark nipples showing a bit through the lightweight fabric. I forced myself to look away, but my shaft grew rock hard anyway, just like always.

"Trevor, I need you to do something, and I don't want you to argue with me." She rubbed her lower back. Maybe she wanted another massage.

A tense kind of awareness niggled at the back of my skull, but after everything we'd been through, I wasn't about to deny her anything. "Sure. What do you need?"

In one shockingly fluid motion, she whisked her nightgown over her head, revealing those bare breasts I'd been attempting not to notice. "I need you to stimulate my nipples."

I blinked several times in a row. Was I dreaming? She wouldn't ask for that. Not now. We hadn't been sexual in an eternity. I hadn't pleasured myself this often since I'd been a teenager. But a guy had to do what a guy had to do. I must've heard her incorrectly, but if I had, why was she exposing herself to me?

"You need what now?" I asked her, my eyes glued to the nipples in question. Christ, they were enormous and dark and delicious looking. *Fuck*.

"I can't take being pregnant anymore. I just can't. I was sound asleep, and the baby still woke me up. I think he's literally running a marathon in there, just jogging around. I can't do this for one more second."

"So you want me to …" I trailed off. I wanted this too badly to trust that's what she'd actually said.

"Stimulate my nipples. Rub them. Stroke them. Massage them. Whatever. I just have to get this show on the road, you know?"

I tamped down my enthusiasm. She wasn't asking me to make love to her. She wasn't horny. She still didn't love me. Not like that. She just wanted me to assist her in getting her labor started. Could I really do this without going too far?

Only one way to find out.

I stepped forward and reached out to touch her, and damn, my hands were trembling with desire.

Nice and easy, Keller.

I tried to approach this like I would a back rub. Find the tight muscles and make them relax. Sure. Except as soon as my palms brushed those pebbled nubs, there was no way to pretend I was touching something as ordinary as her back. Her body responded, her nipples visibly puckering, and I closed my eyes, hoping that would help.

It didn't.

Now, all I could do was give my complete attention to the feel of those incredibly globe-like breasts in my hands. She moaned as my fingers closed around her, shifting so that more of her filled my hold. My breathing accelerated, as did hers. In my best attempt at remaining clinical, I spoke.

"Are they sore like they used to be?" Yeah, that was it. Ask something like a doctor would. Only the response she gave me wasn't nothing like what a patient's would be.

"No. That feels ... uuuuhn ..." She moaned again, and I held my breath. "Suck on them."

"Huh?" was my uber intellectual response.

"Suck them, Trevor."

"Yeah?"

"Please ..."

No way on God's green earth was I saying no to that. So I bent low enough to wrap my lips around her left breast. She made a new sound, one I'd heard her make when we'd been in bed. It was a cross between a moan, a cry, and a keen. It'd always driven me wild, and now was no exception. I nearly came untouched from that alone.

But she wasn't finished.

"More, Trevor. I need more." So I switched to the other, sucking it deeply into my mouth. She tasted so good, like warmth and woman and love.

I banded my arms around her to get a more stable hold, one hand on her back and the other at her hip. Her belly bulged out against mine, but like the last time, knowing she was expecting my child was a turn on rather than a turn off. It made me want to possess her, to hold her, to have her.

I was barely hanging on to my higher brain functions when she undid that, too. "Make love to me, Trevor. Make me yours again."

And that was all she wrote.

Faster than was probably advisable, I swept Jessica's legs out from under her and rushed her over to her bed. I yanked down the bikini panties she wore, and traced a finger amongst her folds, finding her so slick that my balls tightened dangerously.

"Jesus fucking Christ, you're so wet," I said out loud, my mind consumed with lust. I'd never been with a woman so ready for me, not even Jessica herself. She was dripping, for God's sake.

I tore my sweatpants and hoodie off in a flash and reclined on my back on her mattress. Reaching for her, I helped her straddle me. I was just about to ask her if she was okay with riding me when she sank down onto me inch by inch, making my ability to vocalize evaporate as I released a long groan instead.

She created the rhythm she needed, rocking on me more raucously than I would've thought she'd like in her current condition. I held her hips before remembering her specific request, and then drew each of my thumbs along her nipples, squeezing them very gently. The belly restricted many positions, but I was more than willing to let Jessica show me whatever she needed.

"Trevor," she hummed. "Ohhh, Trevor, yes."

Already, she was close. I could feel her inner walls thrumming with a tension that was escalating second by second. I shifted my hips up and down, matching her motions, our rhythm synching flawlessly.

"Trevor?" Her tone was different this time, and I knew she wasn't merely calling out in ecstasy.

"Yeah? You okay?"

"I need to tell you something."

My first instinct was to say, "Now?" But I didn't. I was here for her. I was doing my best to prove to her that I would be whatever she needed. I wanted to show her that I loved her in whichever way she could accept it. The truth was, I was hers. Totally and without question. She slowed, almost stopping.

That didn't bode well.

I swallowed, fearful that she was about to shut this amazing moment down. "What do you need to tell me?"

She stared unwaveringly into my eyes. "It's just that I ..." she trailed off, nearly killing me.

"Yeah?" I prompted her, internally screaming at myself to not thrust upwards.

She leaned forward as far as she could, resting her hands on my cheeks, her thumbs nuzzling my bristly chin. "I love you," she whispered, and then she came.

Because I was so still, I could feel every throb and every pulse. She held my eyes, her jade green irises a thin circle as her lust took her over, and I knew that she meant what she'd said, that she'd forgiven me, that at long last, she was mine.

And that knowledge and the feel of her milking me was more than enough to set off my own orgasm. I pumped into her, my body drawing our both my pleasure and hers. It was glorious, and surprisingly tender in a manner that sex had never been for me.

Sated, she slipped down and slightly off to the side, and I roped my arms around her delectable body.

"Jessica?"

"Mmmm?"

"I love you, too."

I felt her smile against my chest, and I wanted to preserve this moment forever. It was in this serene state of mind that both of us fell asleep.

∼

It was dark when I stirred, but the yellow line of predawn hung right at the horizon out the window. Not my window, but Jessica's. I was in her bed. And she was awake and jostling me. I put out a hand to soothe her.

"Don't have to get up yet. Just relax," I muttered, but then the jostling became harder.

"Um, Trevor?"

"Uh huh." My eyes drifted back closed.

"I can't tell for sure, but I think my water just broke."

That was enough to jolt me out of bed like I'd been electrocuted. "You're in labor?"

"Well, I think so. I've been having these pains every few minutes. At first, I didn't think much of it and went back to sleep, but now they're harder to ignore. And there's this embarrassing stain on my bed now."

I flicked on the lamp and saw a small pool of moisture between her legs. And it wasn't just a sex wet spot, either.

"Uhm, how long do you think it's been since it started?"

"A couple of hours, maybe, for the contractions. The water breaking thing just happened, though."

Okay. I could handle this. We prepared for this. We have a game plan. No problem. So why was the hand I'd just scrubbed down my face trembling. Time to buck up and show Jessica she could depend on me no matter what. I threw on my clothes and shoes.

"So, we need to get to the hospital. Where's your bag?"

"In that corner." She pointed vaguely to the right, and I saw the backpack.

"Cool."

"Owww," she hissed out, clutching her stomach and breathing in short puffy breaths. "That one hurt."

"Dr. Carrey said the contractions needed to be four minutes apart before we left, right?"

"Yeah," she agreed.

"Have you been timing them?"

She nodded. "The last one was five minutes ago."

"Let's get you dressed," I said, opening drawers and closing them. I didn't even know what I was looking for.

"My sweats are in that bottom drawer. Help me up, and I'll get them." Carefully, I held out an arm so she could leverage herself up. She bent over, obviously hurting again. "Ohhh. That one was bad. Like, really bad." She said once it was over.

Screw waiting for the four-minute mark. She was in pain now. I automatically reached into the drawer she'd been heading for, finding a set of pink fleece pants and an oversized maternity t-shirt. I didn't know where her underwear was and frankly, I didn't care. She'd have to strip them off anyway, so what was the point?

Once we were both dressed, I slung her backpack over my shoulder, took her arm and led her step by step toward my SUV. I felt this unsettling combination of a need to rush and an equal need to move with extreme caution. The anxiety of the situation ratcheted up to new heights every time she experienced a contraction.

Even in the past few minutes, they'd grown stronger and closer together. She had another one as we reached the sidewalk outside, and even though she was taking these short little Lamaze breaths, she stopped halfway through and cried out. Jessica had broken out into a sweat now, and I had to get her to the goddamn hospital.

When the contraction released her, she burst into sobs. "I don't know if I can do this, Trevor."

"You can, okay. I know you can. I'm right here, and I'm not going anywhere."

She looked terrified, and I just couldn't take it. So, I scooped her up and carried her straight into the parking garage. She clung to me for dear life, her curly hair tickling my neck, and as I bleeped the locks, I took a split second to look into her face. She glanced up at me, too, and despite the direness of the situation, I knew somehow, everything was going to work out.

"I love you, Jessica. I'm so proud of you. After our son arrives, why don't you move in with me? What do you think?"

Only after I said the words did it occur to me that now might not be the right time to bring this up. Too late, though. My request was already out there.

I watched the emotions cross her face like a parade. First, there was shock, following by concern. Then a radiant smile lifting her mouth and sparkled in her jade eyes.

"Yes," she said.

"Yes, you'll move in with me?" I clarified.

"Yes," she repeated. "I love you, Trevor, and all I've ever wanted is a fam—" But then her smile twisted into a scowl of discomfort.

Another contraction. I breathed with her this time. She was still in my arms outside the passenger side of my vehicle. Her stomach was against my chest, and I could feel the damn contraction squeezing her myself. Jesus.

"Here's my proposition," I said, as I latched on her seatbelt once the contraction passed. "One, we have this baby. Two, we make sure everything is awesome with you both. Three, we move you both into my place. Sound like a plan?"

She was smiling again. "Definitely."

∽

BIRTH ANNOUNCEMENT

Jessica Souza and Trevor Keller are overjoyed to announce the birth of their son, Joshua Trevor Keller. He was born at 11:12am at Mount Sinai Hospital in Manhattan, New York. He weighed seven pounds two ounces and was twenty-one inches long. Both mother and child have been released and are healthy.

EPILOGUE - JESSIE

SEPTEMBER

Every time I peer down into my baby boy's adorable chubby face, I can't believe he's here or that he belongs to me and Trevor. It feels unreal to see Joshua live and in person, even when he's in my arms. His miniscule hand roots around over my heart, and I shift the cup of my nursing bra so he can latch on.

I've gotten better at breastfeeding over these past few weeks. At first, I didn't know if I could do it. My son had a hard time staying attached to the nipple, and I found the whole thing uncomfortable. But now, thankfully, we've found our stride.

"Hey there, gorgeousness," Trevor said as he brought over a microwaveable breakfast croissant and a cup of herbal tea.

He always insists on feeding me before he goes to work. Being here with him in his apartment has made my life so much easier. I don't have to focus on cooking or cleaning or anything but taking care of our baby. And as soon as my man comes home, he takes Joshua so I can rest or jump in the shower. It's been so much better than I once imagined.

"I'm running a little behind, but I wish I didn't have to go, especially on a Saturday," he said, his expression regretful. Trevor has been incredibly attentive. Not only to me, but to our son.

"Me, too, but we'll be fine."

This past Monday I went back to school to finish out my teaching degree, something I'd looked forward to but also dreaded. I'd considered backing out of it a million times, but Trevor always reminded me that Joshua will only be without one of us for a few hours a day. I hated the idea, even though I trusted his new nanny with all my heart.

Ashley will be the one here with him. She graduated last semester, but so far, she hadn't found a job. This solution, though temporary, worked out for all of us.

"Commence Mission Stay Awake," Trevor said, his smile wolfish as he waggled one eyebrow at me.

Since Joshua's birth, he's been giving me pecks on the cheeks, forehead, and the lips, keeping his affections frequent but not overtly amorous. Now, though, he kissed me like he meant it, like the salvation of his soul was on the line. I could relate. Today marked the point of us being able to resume sexual activity, and I couldn't wait. Joshua had just started sleeping through the night, so with any luck, we'd reconnect tonight in every way possible.

I glanced down at our son. He had a head full of dark curly hair and had Trevor's striking amber eyes. He was beautiful beyond measure.

Reluctantly, the man I loved backed away, and if the bulge behind his suit pants was any indication, that lip-lock had made quite an impression on him. "Do me a favor and remember how much I love you two while I'm gone, okay?"

He said this every single day before he left. The sentiment made me glow from the inside out. "Just as long as you do the same."

"Always," he said, as he quietly clicked the door shut behind him. And thanks to Trevor Keller, I would forever know exactly what that word meant.

THE END

PREQUEL TO DAMAGED

THANKS FOR READING Damaged! The Billionaire Secret Club is just getting started. Are you hooked on Jessie and Trevor?

You can read about them here in this special short story.

Then read on for a preview of the next book in The Billionaire Secret Club Series, Off Limits.

Grab Your FREE Book 👉 https://BookHip.com/CZKZKH

OFF LIMITS

A DARK BILLIONAIRE ROMANCE

DAMAGED

C.C. PIPER

1

ALAINA

As I traipsed across the campus at Seattle University, I twisted my infinity ring around my pinky and took in a deep, cleansing breath. The ring had been a graduation gift from my parents, though I suspected my dad had more to do with it than my mom. For years I'd worn it without giving much thought to what that symbol meant. Infinity equaled forever, as in, *I'll love you forever.*

But I knew love tended to be conditional rather than infinite.

Oh, well.

The familiar scents of pine, fir, spruce and redcedar permeated the air, reminding me of my childhood. This was a place so unlike London, where the ever-present odor of exhaust fumes and petrol reigned. Not that living in the heart of

Britain was an urban nightmare or anything. I'd enjoyed residing there over the past three years.

Almost everything about that city was historic with a capital H. London was a fascinating location, and it had been amazing to experience it firsthand. But it couldn't compare to the pristine greenness of the Pacific Northwest. At least, not to me.

I'd returned because I wanted to strike out on my own as an entrepreneur, something far easier to do in America than in England. As an expat, I would've had to jump through about a million different hoops to begin a startup overseas. Doing the same here would still require a lot of effort, but there were more opportunities overall. Opportunities I intended to take advantage of.

On my way to my cute little aqua Mini-Cooper convertible – one I'd purchased while in England – I caught sight of a group of tall men in red jerseys, the Seattle University Redhawks. The Redhawks were the college's Division One basketball team, and they competed frequently in the NCAA championships.

But it wasn't the fact that this mass of admittedly handsome players were eyeing me as they strutted by that caught my attention. What made me do a doubletake was a flash of bright copper hair. I scrutinized them again, narrowing my eyes as I searched for August "Auggie" Cunningham. But the redheaded guy I saw wasn't him. Auggie wouldn't show up nearly five thousand miles away from his beloved alma mater in Oxford, anyway.

My ex-boyfriend was probably too busy boinking my ex-best friend and roommate, Gwen Howard to be thinking about me.

He – or *they* – were the other reason I'd moved back to the States. I'd thought of Gwen as a sister, as my British BFF. And I'd thought Auggie and I would go the distance, as well. We'd made plans as a couple, and since we'd been together for over two years, I'd believed in those plans with all my heart.

I would obtain my British citizenship. We would settle in some quaint cottage just outside of London and commute to work so we'd experience the best of both worlds. We'd discussed getting married sooner rather than later, and we also wanted to start a family within the next three to five years.

But it turned out, Auggie wasn't half as interested in that plan as I was.

I still remembered returning to the flat I shared with Gwen that godawful afternoon. I'd come back home earlier than usual because one of my summer classes had been canceled.

I'd been looking forward to having the place to myself, the peace and quiet would help me develop my newest set of designs for the handbag business I wanted to create.

Then, I'd heard a noise. At first, I didn't think anything of it. We had neighbors all around us, and sometimes they could be loud. But as I headed toward the back of the flat, I realized that the sound had been coming from *our* abode. I called out:

"Gwen? You home?"

As I listened, I heard music. Gwen loved hard rock, the more percussive the better. She sometimes got us into trouble because she liked to play it loudly at all hours of the night. So, other than the fact that she wasn't normally at home at that time of day, I hadn't thought much of it. Not until I heard something banging around in *my* room.

I didn't understand why Gwen would be in my room rather than her own. Was she looking to borrow something? Was she dancing through the entire house?

"Gwen?" I raised my voice again, but the music drowned it out.

The whole situation was just odd enough that I pushed my way past my door to see what was going on. What I saw froze me in my tracks as if I'd been transformed into an ice sculpture.

My boyfriend was plowing into my best friend from behind and the force he was using made the headboard – *my* headboard – crash over and over again into the wall. All I could focus on was their bare, perspiring skin as they continued to go at it doggie style on my bed.

To this day, I couldn't remember saying anything, but I must've shrieked or something because both of them twisted at the same moment in my direction.

"Alaina…" Gwen had sputtered out. "You're home."

No shit, Sherlock.

I'd thought this rather than saying it aloud, though. My mother's nagging comments about a lady never cursing still rang in my ears despite her being so far away.

"This isn't what it looks like, darling," Auggie said next, and I blinked at him.

"What else could it possibly be?"

"Erm…" It was rare for my boyfriend to be at a loss for words, but this time he appeared to be struggling for them. "Okay, it *is* what it looks like, but I can explain."

"Explain, then," I demanded. I didn't know why I wanted him to, but I did.

"We were going to wait to consummate the relationship until we were engaged, right? Well, this was my way of leaving you alone 'till then, of keeping that promise."

Up until that moment, I'd always thought of Auggie as an intelligent man. He was known for having book smarts out the wazoo. But apparently, he'd missed growing some crucial brain cells when it came to common sense and decency. Gwen's minimal decency must've have kicked in because she seemed to decide that disengaging her body from his might be a good idea. After pulling away, she covered herself with my comforter and hid her face in shame.

She'd certainly earned it.

"Are you seriously saying that cheating on me with my best friend equates to you being honorable, somehow?"

His mouth opened and shut a few times, his copper hair glinting in the sunlight coming through the window. They hadn't even bothered to close the blinds. Time slowed to a near stop as I absorbed the catastrophe of the scene. My BFF – *ex*-BFF – cowering to hide herself in my blankets. My boyfriend – *ex*-boyfriend – standing there naked as a jaybird making excuses. I'd never even seen him completely in the buff before that very minute.

How stupid was I?

"Get out," I ground out, surprised at the steadiness of my voice. But neither of them moved. "I said, *get out*." To my knowledge, I'd never sounded so ruthlessly cold before. The amount of hate singing through my system was so high that I was a bit afraid of myself. My blood pressure must've skyrocketed because the tension in my muscles made me feel like I might break.

Auggie stooped to grab up his pile of clothing and backed slowly out of the room. Gwen began to take my comforter with her, until I glared at her so fiercely that she seemed to take the hint. She dropped my bed linens and disappeared into her room across the hall, bolting her door for good measure.

For a long while I simply stood there, breathing in the pong of sex and sweat mixed with his cologne and her perfume. Then, I packed up my things, dialed up a hackney carriage (which at home was called a taxi), and went straight to Heathrow. In the wee hours of the next morning, I found myself in my childhood bedroom on my parents' sprawling estate.

My dad had welcomed me back without prying. Maybe that was why I'd always been a daddy's girl. My mother, on the other hand, responded with twenty questions. One of which was "Alaina, have you gained weight? I don't recall you being this rounded out when we came last Christmas."

Ugh.

Luckily, my father had tugged her out of my room saying he was sure I needed to recover from the lengthy and impromptu trip I'd just taken. A few hours later, I awoke when my brother Andrew poked his head into my room like he did when I was seven and he was fourteen.

"What's up, buttercup?" Andy asked me as he sat on the edge of my frilly double bed. That'd been his nickname for me ever since I could remember.

"Nothing much," I mumbled.

He nudged my knee. "There's no real reason why you upended your life by taking an unscheduled flight home in the middle of the night?"

"Well, I did catch Auggie in bed with my roommate."

His eyes went huge. "Holy fuck! Really?"

I nodded, and I couldn't say why, but it was that action that brought all my emotions to the fore. I sort of collapsed in on myself as I became a weepy bundle of girl. My big brother did his best to console me by patting my back and murmuring quiet words of comfort. I cried for a long time until...

"Want me to go over there and beat him to death with one of those cricket bats?" Andy asked me, and something about the image of that made me giggle like a little kid.

Things got better after that. Except for when I spotted any guy with dark red hair similar to Auggie's.

Guess I needed to work on that.

I hopped behind my steering wheel and accidentally pealed out of the parking lot.

Calm down. It wasn't him, and it never will be.

Too bad telling myself that didn't help much. I did my best to shake off all my wayward thoughts and feelings about my ex as I hurried down the road toward my father's law firm. Daddy and I had a lunch date.

Williams and Chung had been the name of the firm when I left three years ago, but since the elderly Mr. Chung had retired and my brother had been made partner, now it was Williams and Williams. I'd been away when Andy's promotion had come through, though I'd sent him a congratulatory gift. Once I arrived in front of the gray five-floor building downtown, I happened upon someone pulling out of their space.

Score! Parking was usually in the vicinity of impossible this time of day. Looked like maybe the Fates were peering down at me with more kindness all of a sudden. Lord knew I'd had enough crappy luck lately to last me a good long while.

The day was unfettered by rain or clouds, and while that was nice, it meant I had to shade my eyes with my hands as I glanced upward. Another name had been added to the outside façade in brilliant golden lettering, but the glare meant I had to squint to read it. I rushed over the concrete curb with my gaze still fixed on the placard above me.

Williams, Williams, and K...

"Ooomph," I grunted out as I collided with something as solid as a brick wall. I fell back a pace, nearly losing my balance and taking a header, when a large hand reached out and snatched me from death's grip. Okay, death's grip might be a bit dramatic, but if I'd taken that tumble it would've hurt.

A lot.

Grasping onto a surprisingly sturdy arm considering it was clad in a high-end suit, I peeked up into the face of my savior. His dark chestnut hair was just long enough to slip over his forehead, and his square jaw was covered with delectable scruff. He had full yet firm lips, a straight nose, and chocolate brown eyes. These recognizable features had made frequent appearances in my dreams since the tender age of sixteen. And at this angle, I was also able to make out the last name on the façade.

King. As in Mason King. My brother's best bud. Someone I'd known all my life. At some point during my three-year absence, he'd apparently made partner, too, though I didn't recall anyone telling me.

Mason had been my secret and most agonizing crush for what amounted to an eternity, and I'd literally run right into him.

Dear Lord, kill me now.

2

MASON

"Buttercup? Is that you?"

She huffed. "I genuinely and sincerely wish you and Andy wouldn't call me that in public."

I grinned as I peered down at my best friend's baby sister, not bothering to disguise my astonishment. The last time I'd seen Alaina Williams, it had only been for the briefest second as I'd hurried to catch my flight to San Francisco to finish Law School.

That had been five years ago.

I always thought of her as she was when I'd left for college. Back then, she couldn't have been more than twelve, wearing braces and a perpetual – yet adorable – blush. Back then, I was a youthful college undergrad without a care in the world. I stayed so busy having a good time, I didn't give her much thought again.

Well, that's a lie. I *had* thought about her at times. But not in any type of creepazoid fashion. I'd always liked her. When she relaxed around me, she was quite a hoot. Goofy, creative and innocent. She was the type of kid who laughed easily and wrote things down on the inside of her arm so she wouldn't forget. I'd found these quirks of hers charming. Charming and sweet, if naïve.

My first years as an attorney had been spent in San Francisco. Then, I moved back to Seattle, the town Andy, Alaina and I had all been born and raised in, while she was still in London. But I'd had no idea that she'd changed so much. Matured so much.

That cute and slightly awkward teenager had been replaced by this young yet far-too-attractive woman. We still had a hold of one another, and I realized that every place we remained in physical contact was tingling in a rather noteworthy way. An enticing way. An *arousing* way.

Shit!

Back off from your bro's kid sister, asshole.

I released her, and she stumbled backwards. So, I grabbed her, thrust her up off the worrisome curb, and let go of her once she was safe again. *Sheesh*.

Although she was no longer in my arms, I couldn't seem to tear my eyes from her. Her long wavy blond hair had been swept up into a messy bun, and the flyaway tendrils that drifted along her creamy neck were doing strange things to me. So were the understated gold earrings she wore that dangled beneath her earlobe and caught the light whenever she moved. And so were her bow-shaped lips and hazel eyes.

Those eyes were so fascinating. Deep blue along the outside, a lighter bluish green on the inside, and a starburst of brown around her pupils. The aromatic essence of something floral drifted around her and over to me, and I inhaled the heady fragrance. Then, on top of all that, there was her body.

Good God.

Her figure had become this shapely hourglass. The simple short-sleeved Seattle University t-shirt she had tucked into her skinny jeans this warm September day only served to accentuate this.

Let me say it again.

Good *God.*

Then, from directly behind me, came one of the two men I most didn't want privy to my current thoughts.

"Ready for lunch, sweetheart?" said Bryant Williams, the senior partner of my law firm and Alaina and Andy's father.

"Sure, Daddy. I've been hungry for that sushi all morning."

"Let's get to it, then. Mason, you two get a chance to catch up?" he asked me, and I surreptitiously cleared my throat.

"Well, we just sort of bumped into each other."

"Literally," Alaina put in, a small grin lighting her features. The braces were gone, and her smile was perfect and white. Beautiful. Especially since that smile was highlighted by those rosy lips of hers. Unlike many of my recent dates, Alaina was tall, only a few inches shorter than my own six three. It put us on more even ground, lining us up, which I liked.

Yeah, she's in an awesome position for smooching the living daylights out of me, my traitorous lizard brain chimed in.

Shut up, you horny bastard.

"I'll be taking her off your hands for now," Bryant said, putting an image of my hands all over her in my head.

What the ever-loving fuck was the matter with me?

"Excellent," I replied in a higher pitch than usual. "Have fun."

He waved, led his daughter to his Mercedes sedan, and zoomed off. I stood there staring after them, even once the car had vanished around the corner. Andy had mentioned her return, but I hadn't expected her to morph into someone so captivating she might be asked to walk a runway at any moment.

That idea threw an image of her in a swimsuit into my mind. Maybe one of those barely-there bikinis. My phone went off, and relief flooded me. I welcomed the distraction. A quick glimpse showed me the person on the other end of the line was a colleague of mine who I'd been friendly with for years, Trevor Keller.

"Trevor. Haven't heard from you in eons, dude. How are you?"

"Fabulous, man. Really great. My little boy is six months old now, and I got engaged to his mom last weekend," he answered.

"Seriously?" I asked him, wondering if he was yanking my chain.

Trevor had been a terminal bachelor ever since I'd known him. The man didn't even date except through a service that provided paid escorts. I knew this because he and a couple of my other business associates, Richard Boswell and James Carter, had ties to the woman in charge of the same "club." She liked to stay anonymous by going by the somewhat ridiculous moniker of the Wish Maker.

I didn't know what to make of the whole concept, honestly.

"Seriously. I'm happy as a clam. You should try it."

Whether he meant I should enlist the Wish Maker's services, become spontaneously happy, get engaged or have a kid remained a mystery I had no desire to clarify. "How about I leave all that to you?"

He laughed. "If you insist. I'm reaching out to see if you might like to throw your ring into an investment opportunity I just heard about. It's low risk and has an amazing ROI."

"They all do." Trevor could sell anything to anybody. It was his unique gift upon this planet. I enjoyed giving him a hard time about this, but the truth was that he'd made me money every time I'd agreed to go in on a project with him. Like, six figure money. "What's the deal this time?"

As he explained all the ins and outs of his current opportunity, I traversed the short distance to my Escalade and closed my door so I could hear him better. In the end, I agreed to invest. He hadn't led me wrong yet. Still, I couldn't imagine him as a husband and father. It went against everything I knew about him.

"So, you're all about the big life changes, huh?" I asked him. He did sound happy, and I found that intriguing.

"A year and a half ago, I was this miserable son of a bitch who worked so many hours at the bank I almost bought a pullout sofa to keep in my office. But then," his tone altered to one I could only describe as peaceful and content. "I met Jessica, and all the holes in my life filled right up, you know? It's incredible. You got anyone yourself?"

I hesitated to answer this time. Trevor and I didn't know each other tremendously well, so he didn't know about my past. He didn't know that the one and only time I'd taken a chance on love it'd ended in the worst outcome possible. I made a vow to never go down that path again.

Never ever.

Loving others deeply meant losing them could destroy you. Even now, grief hovered over me like a specter as if lying in wait to strike again. It was a risk I was no longer willing to take. Keeping things surface level was the safest bet. That's why I'd become a one-and-done type of guy. Too bad I hadn't even enjoyed one of those in several months.

"I'm guessing by your silence that you don't," Trevor interrupted my dark musings. "You should call up the Wish Maker, man. Not for anything serious, if that's not your thing. But just for fun. Tell her your type and let her know your preferences for the date itself. She'll take care of the girl, the activities you go on, any accommodations you might need. You should do it. Everyone needs some stress relief now and again."

"Sounds like your stress relief became something else entirely," I quipped, half-joking, but his tone said he wasn't kidding around.

"I didn't think anything real could ever be on the cards for me, even though that's what I was truly after. Now, I have Jessica and my son Joshua. I wake up in the morning, look around and ask how I got so lucky."

I hadn't anticipated that our business conversation would take such a personal turn, but I had to admit that he had piqued my inquisitive nature. "Fine. Text me the woman's number. Maybe I'll give her a call."

"You won't regret it," Trevor promised, then he disconnected. I received the text seconds later. I looked at the ten digits, knowing how insane this sounded.

Was I really going to do this? Procrastinating, I hit my push button ignition and started the engine. I sat there in the covered parking garage beside our firm, weighing up my options. I'd trusted Trevor before, and all I was looking for was a good time. I didn't have anything as vital as a wife and child riding on this. I just needed an evening out on the town followed by some possible sexy times if everything went down right.

What could it hurt?

Want to read more? Get Off Limits HERE!

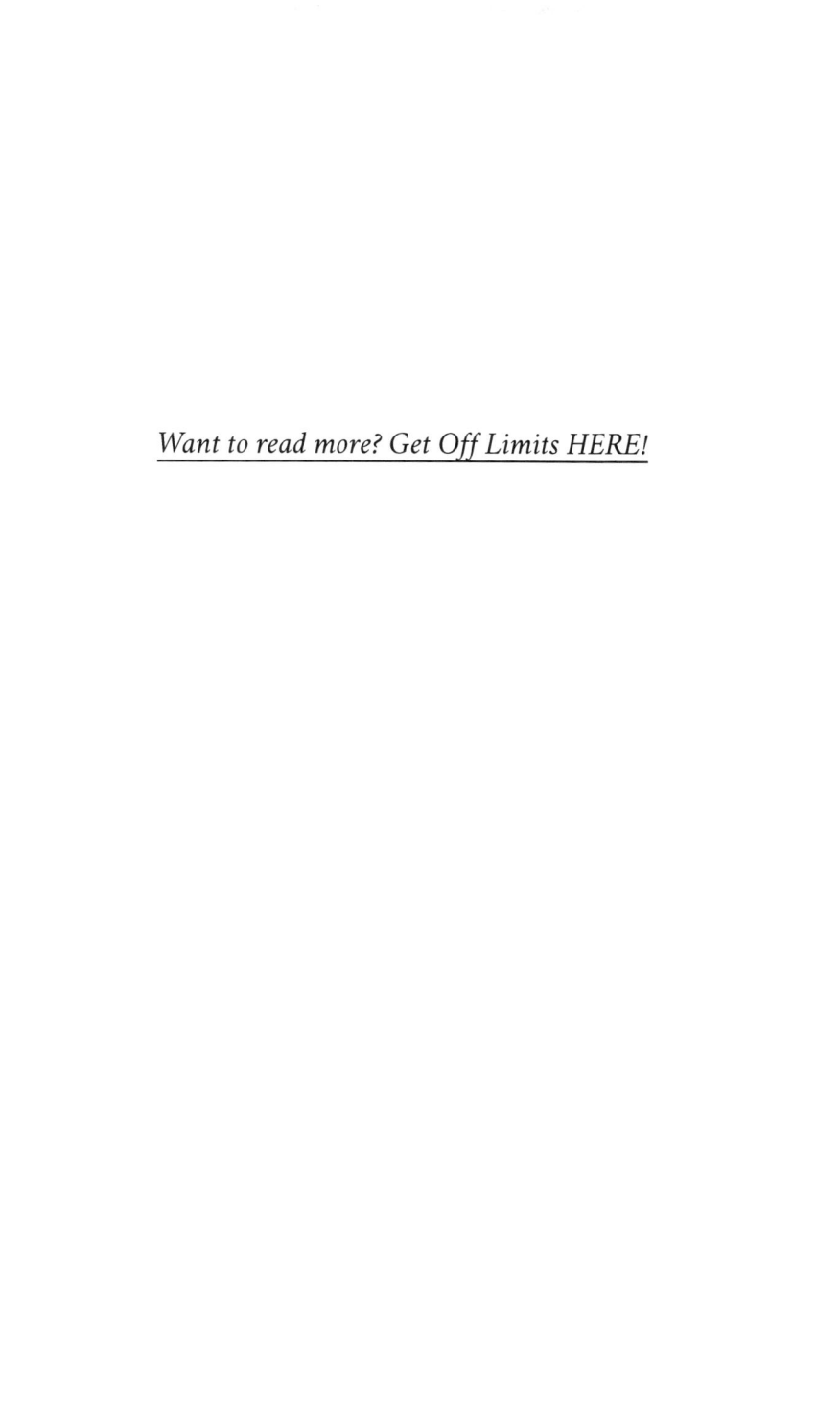

Printed in Great Britain
by Amazon